Mate Match

Savanna Golden

Contents

ISBN-13: 979-8-9914457-1-9

Imprint: Independently Published

Cover design by: Savanna Golden via Canva

Printed in the United States of America

To my husband, for always indulging in my crazy ideas and supporting my ambitions.

To the Booktok community, for sharing your love of reading.

Prologue

FINLEY

The cafe on the main street is teeming with enthusiastic patrons. As I sip my ice chai latte my best friend Kai is recounting how she spent the previous evening. She spent the night on a date she met via an app that caters to supernaturals. I enjoy haranguing her about using such a resource to meet people. She often likes to point out that at least she is going out on dates rather than living a solitary life like me, as well as detailing the reasons that it is helpful to be able to determine that your date is supernatural like us rather than a human.

"I'm telling you, Finley, this app is a game changer!" Kai all but yells as she tries to rebuke the argument, I made only moments ago against the idea. I give her a side eye as I take another sip. "Don't you dare judge me Finley, I'm tired of waiting for someone from the pack to notice how amazing I am and decided

I would expand my horizons to include possibilities outside of shifters."

Our pack, Fang, is one of the most prestigious groups of wolf shifters in America. In general, shifters are one the supernaturals with the lowest numbers, partly because it is something you need to be born into unlike some types of supernaturals like the vamps, but I think it is also because not all shifters can keep their wits about them in their animal form and tend to have an early mortality. Fang has the highest concentration of shifters in one pack. Despite our population and that it is rare for shifters to look outside of our species for a mate it still doesn't guarantee that there's someone for everyone.

"Alright I'll humor you for a moment, but probably not long", I chuckle. "What is the name of this app you have been raving about?" I give her my full attention, so she knows that I don't begrudge her for her interest.

"Give me your phone", she reaches over and snatches it, "I'll download it for you." I tried to prevent her hand from curling around my phone, but I was too slow when I was silently debating whether I wanted to order another drink. I have a feeling I will need the extra caffeine today.

After a minute she hands me back my phone and I look down at my screen to see what she added. She already has the app, Mate Match, open and I see a black background with red flaming hearts, the company logo in stark contrast.

"Kai, this looks extremely cheesy", I tell her as I shoot her a disapproving glare. She rolls her eyes and shakes her head causing her platinum blond hair to fly wildly around her. "I'm going to be deleting this!" She immediately knocks my phone out of my hand and yells, "Don't you dare!"

My phone hits the table with a loud *thunk*, and both phones simultaneously ping. We exchange a look of intrigue, and both grab our phones. It is a new text message from the head of pack communications. I almost dropped my phone when I saw the message.

> **Alpha Angus MacGregor has passed to the beyond. A new alpha will be determined at the next full moon gathering.**

Tears start to gather in the corner of my eyes before I raise my head to see if Kai has also finished reading the message we received. Angus has been the alpha my entire life and according to some of the older pack members he's been one of the best leaders since the formation of Fang. Not only did he lead our pack, but he played a large role in my life while I was growing up since I was close with his children. He had three sons–Callum, Fallon, and Knox. His middle son Fallon is the same age as me and we grew up being inseparable. He was my best friend for most of my life until things got very complicated and messy.

Kai finally seems to shake out of her stupor and asks, "Who do you think it will be?" I shrug my shoulders trying to feign nonchalance, but I'm nervous about the possibilities. Every alpha of our pack has been from the MacGregor family, so it stands to reason that the next alpha will be one of Angus' sons.

The alpha role does not necessarily go in birth order so it could be any one of the three or someone else if they challenge and win.

After a few more minutes of trying to regain some sense of casual demeanor, we decide to call it quits and go our separate ways. The news we received ended up changing the mood for both of us and it wasn't worth trying to continue with our original plans.

That evening as I lie in bed, unable to achieve sleep, I think about all that has happened today. I grab my phone and think about something that might distract me. I decide to delete the app Kai downloaded but when I bring it up, I can't stop myself from being mildly curious. Before I even could give it much thought, I decided to create a profile. Just to be nosey. I seriously have no plans of actually utilizing it. I fill in all the required information about myself and by the end, I'm feeling much more fatigued. I plug my phone in for the night and as I start drifting to sleep, I think, nothing is going to come from this, it's not like I'm looking for love.

One

FINLEY

F*ive Years Ago*

I pull up to the MacGregor house and notice how many cars are there, it instantly puts me in a foul mood. Earlier today Fallon had texted me with an invitation to hang out tonight to celebrate my recent 18th birthday. He said it would just be us, but people are streaming out from everywhere. This night of games, talking, and quality time with my best friend appears to have morphed into a full-on rager. I'm not sure how this would have happened, neither Fallon nor I are big on parties.

It takes me a few minutes but eventually, I find a place to park my car and slam my door shut. I start marching up to the house, radiating tension, and on my way inside I run smack into Callum—Fallon's older brother. Callum is two years older and extremely handsome. I've spent years secretly pining for him. My mood instantly goes from ire to flustered as he grabs me around the waist to keep me from falling over after our collision. He looks me in the eye, smiles, and yells, "Birthday Girl!" He waits for a beat with his hands still lingering on my waist while peering at me expectantly. I finally realize I should probably give some sort of acknowledgment to him rather than continue to stare at him like a love-struck puppy. "Hey Callum", I finally stammer out while trying to not think about the flush of color that has surely taken over my cheeks. He grins even larger than before and I'm sure he can probably see the effect he has on me, clearly displayed on my face.

He releases my waist and takes a step back. I look up at him and apologize for running into him, blaming the incident on my poor coordination. I look around at the crowd as loud music blares in the background. "I didn't realize anything was happening here tonight. Fallon messaged me earlier to come over to hang out and celebrate my birthday." He gives a little chuckle and says, "Oh I'm aware of why you're here. My little brother told me you would be celebrating tonight but when he told me what he had planned I thought you deserved something grander. I sent out a few calls to friends and now the party is in full swing." He gestures widely around the party and says, "Happy birthday!"

"You're responsible for this mayhem?"

He smirks at me and says, "Most definitely." He wraps me in a quick hug and then tells me he has a few things to handle. He points to the backyard and says, "All the drinks are out back." He walks away without another word.

Instead of heading to the backyard as he alluded to, I hastily walk into the front of the house. I narrow my eyes as I scan around for Fallon. If anyone is going to be able to make sense of what I'm witnessing it will be him.

Standing in the foyer I can distantly hear Fallon shouting at someone and follow his voice to the dining room. Two guys are standing on the very large dining room table wrestling and poor Fallon is trying to rein in the chaos. He is yelling at both guys and also trying to pull the closest one off the table, but it doesn't seem to be penetrating the idiots' brains. I walk quickly to the table and yell, "Hey dumbass one and two get the hell off the table!" I grab the arm of one man while Fallon grabs the other man's arm, and we thankfully pry them apart. I give them both a withering glare and tell them, "Go find something less destructive to do or leave." I didn't expect them to listen as I am no one of any authority however, they both go their separate ways.

Fallon wraps me in a tight hug and gives me thanks for helping him with the situation. I shoot daggers at him with my eyes and ask, "Fallon, what the heck is happening? Who are all these people and why are they in your house?" He gives me a placating smile, it in no way has any happy feeling behind it and sheepishly says, "Hey, I'm sorry about all this. Callum stopped by earlier and when he heard we had plans for your birthday he kind of just hijacked everything. He insisted that it would be a perfect opportunity to host a party while Mom and Dad are out of town. I tried telling him we didn't want any part of this, but he insisted he wanted to throw a party for your birthday. Next thing I know he's making call after call and suddenly there's this giant rager happening."

We stand there a few minutes exchanging ideas on how to break this up when Callum pokes his head from the hallway. He stalks over to us and says, "Come on Finley, it's time to come enjoy your party. Time to start mingling." He tries to grab my hand, but I deny him and explain with exasperation that I want no part in all this. He doesn't seem to like that answer, his response is to throw me over his shoulder and walk straight to the backyard. Fallon trails behind us the entire time yelling at Callum to put me down.

Callum walks to a table that is set up as the designated party bar. He grabs a shot and turns to me expectantly, holding it out to me. I try to argue with him I don't want it and that I'm too young to be drinking since it is illegal. After several minutes of him pestering me, I finally grab the shot and throw it back. I almost barf. Gagging, I ask, "What was that?" He doesn't seem inclined to answer, instead, he says, "What not a fan?" I respond with, "Definitely not!" I don't find any humor in this, but he gives a deep laugh and reaches to grab something else. He turns back to me with a plastic cup and pushes it into my hand.

"I don't want this." He doesn't seem to care as he continues to hold the cup firmly in my hand. "Finley," he says my name with such deference that it takes me aback for a moment. He continues with, "Do you trust me?" I look him over for a few seconds before nodding slowly. He gives a small smile and says, "I know my brother had a lame night planned for you guys, but

I wanted you to let loose and have a little fun for once. It's beer. It isn't very strong stuff. Drink it."

"I'm not so sure about this, Callum." He makes a slight frown and tells me, "Finley, nothing bad will happen if you decide to have a little fun for a change. I'm here with you, I'll keep you safe. You trust me, right? I won't let anything bad happen to you. If that isn't enough just remember Fallon is also here and you know he will be playing hall monitor."

I glance at Fallon; he shakes his head and releases a little irritated huff. I turn back to Callum, he smiles, waggles his brows at me, and says, "Please Finley, it'll be fun, I promise." I stand there in silent contemplation for a minute before ultimately taking the plastic cup. I bring the cup to my mouth and start drinking. Callum has his eyes locked on mine in a quiet challenge holding my gaze until I finish the alcohol. He grins approvingly at me.

When I set the empty cup down Callum grabs my hand and yanks me toward the crowd, tossing a, "See you later Fallon", behind us.

The next few hours pass by quickly. I've met several of Callum's friends who attend University with him, they all have been nice to me, and they all have personalities that make you feel like you've always been part of their group. We played a few different yard games together as a team and beat out some of our competition. We danced under the stars first to music that felt jovial and freeing, then to hip-hop music that ended with us dancing much closer together. That was quite the experience. Now we are sitting on top of a patio table at the back of the yard. It's quiet and the night is warm with a comforting breeze, it would be peaceful if it wasn't for all the ruckus coming from the party.

Callum is sitting with his leg resting right against mine. I think this is the closest we have ever sat while spending time together. To be honest this is the first time we have ever spent any time together that didn't include Fallon. Fallon has been my best friend as long as I can remember, and I've never come to their house to see anyone other than him. Callum turns his torso toward me and says, "I have a question I've been pondering for some time." I look him in the eyes and say, "What do you want to know?" He looks at the ground for a second, he looks a little shy which is not his normal behavior, "Have I ever had a chance?" I tilt my head to the side, I'm a little confused by his question, "A chance at what?" He gives me this look, almost like he doesn't comprehend that I have no clue what he is asking, "A chance with you, Finley." I immediately look at my feet, and my face starts feeling flush again, if it wasn't so dark outside, I'm sure he would see it. I am a little nervous, so my answer comes out quieter than I intended, "Of course, you have a chance, Callum."

A smile spreads across his face suddenly but almost as quickly as it appeared it disappears, "What about Fallon?" I scrunch up my eyebrows, again I'm not quite sure what he is getting at. He must realize I don't understand because he amends his question, "Do you have something going on with my brother? Romantically I mean. You two are usually together and I have liked you for a while, but I was unsure what you have with him." I don't mean to, but I unintentionally jerk back, I scrunch up my face, the idea is mildly repulsive to me. I look him in the eye and say, "Fallon is my best friend of course we spend a lot of time together. He is like a brother to me, the idea that anyone would think we had any type of romantic involvement is … I don't even know how to explain it, just know it is not like that at all. I care greatly for him but like I said not in a more than-friends type of way. In all honesty, I've had a thing for you for several years." At this unintended revelation, I feel pretty embarrassed, I didn't imagine I would ever tell Callum how I felt about him. I always thought I'd be the silly little girl who hangs out with his brother, secretly crushing on him and never telling a soul about my feelings.

He must be happy with my answer because he slowly slides his hands into my hair, cradling my head, and lowering his face to mine. I can feel the air from his exhale against my mouth before he leisurely leans closer and places a tentative kiss on my lips. It wasn't a lingering kiss, and it was very gentle, but I never would have anticipated this happening outside of my dreams. When he pulls back, he wraps an arm around my shoulders, I let my body lean into his and rest my head on his shoulder. I might be eighteen, but this is the first kiss I've ever had, and my heart feels like it's grown wings.

***

I sit up and feel extremely groggy. I don't remember falling asleep. I am lying in Fallon's bed, tucked in with his comforter. If I'm in Fallon's bed, where is he? I sit up, stretch, and take a look around in the dark. I find Fallon sleeping across the room on his lumpy futon. I'm not sure how it came to be that I am here sleeping but at least I am somewhere I feel safe and that no one else was in the bed, that would have been awkward. A couple of drinks I've had are catching up with my bladder, so I get up and head to the bathroom down the hall.

When I'm heading back to Fallon's room a pair of arms wrap around me from behind and grab me. It startled me and I let out a little nervous yelp. Callum lets out a little chuckle, "Sorry babe, I didn't mean to scare you. I saw you walking and decided to take this opportunity." I turn in his arms so that I'm facing him and ask, "Take what opportunity?" He says, "For this", then picks me up and walks with me to his room. He places me on his bed while standing in front of me. He reaches out and cups my face and kisses me. This time is surer than earlier in the night. This kiss isn't a gentle touch of our lips. He is kissing me with so much feeling. The kiss is firmer and more insistent, he slides his tongue into my mouth. I'm not sure what to do so I try to follow his lead. I think I'm doing okay kissing him back because he seems to enjoy it and he lets out a low groan. We spend a few minutes kissing like this, and it feels like being in a fire but without getting burned. I feel warm, excited, and hungry for more. He pulls away from the kiss, tucks me under the covers, snuggles close, and says, "Let's go back to sleep." He places a kiss on the top of my head as we drift away.

***

It's the afternoon the next day and while I'm snacking in the kitchen Fallon asks, "Where did you go last night?" My cheeks heat up and I turn away to hide my inflamed face. I think for a minute about how I might explain what happened. I'm not sure how Fallon would feel if he knew I made out with his brother or that there might be something going on between him and me. Before I have too much time to think about it, Callum walks over and without hesitation wraps his arms around me. He places a kiss on my cheek and says, "Morning babe." He is grinning hugely right now and then turns to look at his brother, "She stayed the night in my room." I feel like the look he is giving his brother is provoking, but I don't know why. Fallon is my best friend, if anything he will be disgusted by this situation but other than that I can't see him giving any other type of reaction to his brother's statement.

I look from Callum to Fallon and see rage come across Fallon's face. He stares at his brother, and I've never seen him look this way in all the years I've known him. "What is he talking about Finley? Why would you stay the night sleeping in my brother's room?" Callum looks his brother in the eyes and says, "We're together now, so of course she was going to stay in my room. Right, babe?" We never discussed with him asking me to be his girlfriend or anything even though it was clear we both expressed our feelings for each other but if he is telling Fallon we are a couple I guess that is self-explanatory. I give a noncommittal sort of, "Right."

Fallon looks from his brother to me, and I never would have expected his face to be so angry. He's never been like this toward me before. He huffs out, "Unbelievable", then throws his mug into the sink with such strong force it shatters, sending pieces of broken glass raining out onto the surrounding countertop. Then he walks away.

Two

FINLEY

I'm hard at work when I get smacked in the face with a wadded-up ball of paper. I look up from the design project I'm working on and see Kai glaring at me from across the worktable. After college starting a business with my best friend sounded great. Kai studied marketing, so she does all the social media and promotions for clients; I have a fine arts degree with a major in photography and a minor in graphic design, so I handle all things image-based for our projects. We work great together and have had a windfall success in our company. The only disadvantage to working with Kai is that I can't ever hide anything from her, we are either spending free time together or working together, and she is my constant.

"What was that about?" I ask her. She rolls her eyes and huffs, "I've been trying for over ten minutes to get your attention. I have been talking and you haven't even acknowledged that we are in the same room." I try to give her a small assuaging smile, but my shoulders fall a little, "I'm sorry. I'm kind of in my head today. But I'm listening now, what were you trying to talk to me about?"

She fiddles with a few of the documents on her desk before looking back in my direction, "I was asking you how you felt about the funeral tomorrow. Do you think you will be un-scathed?" I was hoping we wouldn't have to discuss this topic but seeing as the funeral for Angus is tomorrow it's been pretty much the only thing I've been consistently worrying about. I've never met my father, and growing up with Fallon being my best friend, Angus was the father figure in my life. We haven't been as close these past few years, but he still always checked in on me from time to time.

I shrug trying to make myself appear unaffected, she knows better but she lets me get away with the behavior. "I don't know what to expect or how to feel. I feel devastated about Angus. You also know that I've been trying to avoid run-ins with both Fallon and Callum for the past few years and that will be unavoidable at their father's funeral. Knowing I will have no choice but to see them and possibly interact with them is stressing me out. On the other hand, this isn't about me, so I am just going to try to focus on the main situation at hand."

She gives a nod and doesn't press me further for more in-formation. I know if anyone understands it is Kai. We were in college together when all hell broke loose. She was there when I was picking up my life and trying to put back together my broken devastated heart. She saw all the dark parts that followed one of the worst pains I've ever experienced.

Done with work for the day, she starts to gather up her purse and coat, before leaving she says, "I'll pick you up at 10 tomorrow for the funeral. Love you."

***

Closing my front door, I walk out into the dreary gray day walking toward the silver SUV parked at the curb in front of my house. My car is in the shop right now, so Kai was more than happy to pick me up this morning, she said it gave her an excuse to spend more time enjoying her newly purchased vehicle. Secretly I'm glad I had an excuse not to drive, I am not sure how today's event and company are going to affect my mood and functionality. I cross my yard with leaves crunching under my black boots and hop into her SUV.

As I buckle her hand shoots in my direction, "I brought you a coffee, thought you might need the extra oomph to survive today." I accept the coffee gratefully and give her a small nod of thanks as I take a sip. I'm sure the coffee isn't going to be the Band-Aid I need for today, but I happily drink it, at least maybe it will help with my exhaustion. I haven't gotten restful sleep this past week.

Despite the melancholy, the funeral turned out to be beautiful. So many people have come to lay Angus to rest and give his family condolences. I held it together for the burial and the majority of the service following but during the multiple moving eulogies that were given I couldn't stop the tears from falling like a waterfall down my face. All the speeches are complete, things are wrapping up, and now it's time to join the line that is proceeding to give condolences on the way out of the building. I used a small mirror from my purse to check my eye makeup to make sure I didn't have black under my eyes from the eyeliner or mascara I wore. Tucking the mirror away I stand with Kai and join the procession.

The first member of the MacGregor family I encounter is Angus' wife, Rowan. She stands there garbed in a long flowing black dress, her auburn hair in long ringlets. Rowan is in her fifties, and she is still one of the most beautiful women I've ever seen. She has big whiskey-colored eyes and porcelain skin. As she finishes up with the couple ahead of me, I slowly walk over to her. Despite the misery on her face, there is also a wistful expression when her eyes meet mine. At one point she was to be my mother-in-law, and she had always treated me as her daughter. I walk closer and she wraps me in a tight hug almost like she is trying to communicate all the words that haven't been said over the years. We quietly converse before I decide it is time to say goodbye so she can move on to the other waiting friends and family.

Turning toward the door I start walking quickly thinking maybe I could sneak out the front without ever having a run-in with the MacGregor boys. About five feet from the exit that idea comes to a crashing halt as I see all three of them standing right by the door. I guess there is no avoiding this situation. Kai gives me a slight shove toward the door, bringing me out of my head. I walk closer, stopping in front of them. I don't feel like dealing with this, but it seems inevitable, so I look at Knox, being sure to only make eye contact with him I say, "I'm sorry for your loss. Your dad was a great man, and he will truly be missed."

Knox lights up a little bit when he sees me. He steps closer and hugs me. I hug him back, with Knox being significantly shorter than his brothers, and my chin rests on his shoulder. Both Callum and Fallon are looking at me with Knox, one wears an unreadable expression while the other has tension rolling off him in waves. We spend a few minutes catching up and then releasing each other. As I start to walk away a hand grabs my wrist halting my forward progress. Without looking back, I know who stopped me, I would recognize his touch anywhere, I've spent a long time trying to forget the way his hands felt on my body. I've tried and mostly failed at freeing myself of those memories that haunt me.

He steps closer and whispers near my ear, "You were just going to leave and not even say anything to me?" When Callum spoke, I could feel his breath like a caress, and it ignited emotions I'd rather keep buried. I pull out of his grip, and as I stride toward the door, I look over my shoulder and say, "Yep, that's exactly what I had planned."

***

After the intensity of the day, I couldn't have anticipated my current situation. Here I am taking shots like a college frat boy with Kai at a local nightclub that specifically caters to supernaturals.

"Oooh, what about this one?" Kai asks while sliding my phone toward me. A few shots into our evening she decided to go through my notifications for the dating app I joined. I didn't plan to use it, but a lot of people have had interest. She has been having a blast showing off all the profiles and giving her input.

"A squatch, really Kai? You think I'm interested in dating a Sasquatch?" I give her an incredulous look and she replies with a sheepish smile.

"They are way too hairy!" I don't intend to yell that but in my current state, it comes out far louder than intended. "Shh!" We both start cackling. I steal the phone back and scroll through some of the options. After a few swipes I pause for a second, I turn the phone to her showing her a super-hot vampire. He is 26 years old and 6'2", which is a whole foot taller than me, and I honestly am digging that. Reading through his profile you can tell he has a sense of humor. He could be perfect for me. Kai's eyes go wide, she gives me an enthusiastic grin and yells, "Yes! Go for it!"

I hit the connect button and sent a preliminary message to get the ball rolling. For all I know he could be uninterested in me or wolf shifters, but I won't know until I shoot my shot.

"Done," I exclaim and tuck my phone back into my handbag. Grabbing Kai's hand, I drag her out to the dance floor, and we spend the rest of our night there having the time of our lives.

Three

FINLEY

Four Years Ago

Rain drizzles against my windshield, I take a second to check my GPS while I'm at the stop light. The closer I get to my destination the more nervous I feel. I am not sure of the cause.

Callum and I have been together for a year and things got serious quickly. A month ago, Callum proposed to me, and I was completely shocked, but I love him more than anything and of course, want to spend the rest of my life with him. I knew he was intent on us being together long term, but I was surprised that he proposed marriage, not just because of the length of our relationship but also because it isn't as common among supernatural beings to marry. Usually, supes take a mate instead of the human marriage ceremony. Most people who marry do not intend to separate or divorce but it is still possible. With a mating, once the bonding ceremony takes place it is unbreakable. The bond changes you so irrevocably that it even changes your life span if you choose a mate who is not your species. The bond will always shorten the lifespan of whichever being has the longer expectancy, so if one of you has the lifespan equivalent to a human and the other is immortal, it will shorten the life of the one who should have been immortal. This magic helps protect us from the ultimate heartbreak of losing our mate.

I was confused about why he would ask me to marry him rather than to be his mate, but he had some valid points. Callum said with us both being wolf shifters our expected lifespan is the same, so we don't need the bond magic to change our life expectancy. He also said he would only be technically expected to take a mate if he were to become the pack leader. Technically all pack leaders are only given a short time frame to acquire a mate, I never really agreed with this ruling, but it isn't my place to worry about it. Someday when his father dies it might be something we have to worry about but even then, it would be a one out of three odds because he has two brothers.

At first, I was a little bummed that he asked me to marry him rather than the alternative but ultimately, I accepted and was grateful that he wanted to keep me around forever.

My GPS indicates that I'm arriving at my destination. It took a few loops around the lot before I found a parking space.

Tonight, Callum's fraternity is hosting an end-of-semester party. I originally told him that I wouldn't be able to attend but my evening class let out early. We don't attend the same schools and it is about a thirty-minute drive from my school to his. If my class had gotten out at normal time, by the time I cleaned up and made it here there wouldn't be much point to coming over. But with getting out early I decided to surprise him.

After my class got out, I stopped by my dorm and dressed to the nines. My brown hair was styled in big loose curls. My body squeezed into a sexy black cocktail dress. I wore my favorite black heels. I was feeling fierce and couldn't wait to have his eyes roam my entire body.

Music is thumping so loud it's hard to tell the guy at the door who I am, but he ultimately lets me in. There are people everywhere! I hate large gatherings like this, but this scene fits like a snug glove for Callum. He thrives on the energy of parties.

Finally getting tired of searching I asked around if anyone had seen him and a couple of guys pointed me in the direction he was last seen. Heading in that direction I come to a dead stop at what I see in front of me. Callum. He has some chick up against the wall, her legs wrapped around his hips, her arms wrapped around his neck. One hand is squeezing her breast, and the other is under her ass holding her up while he grinds against her. They are making out with abandon; it is sloppy and passionate.

My eyes start burning and I just stand there feeling dumb-struck. The guy I talked to yells, "Yo, Cal!" That causes him to detach his mouth from the woman and he turns looking for the source of the shout. He looks first at the man and then slowly realizes I'm standing there. You can see the moment he realizes what he has done. His face gets a total look of *Oh Shit!*

Tears are trailing down my face and I feel myself struggling for air. I think I'm starting to have a panic attack. All these people in this place standing around staring is making it feel suffocating. I turn and run out the door. Callum keeps yelling my name as I leave but I can't even turn back and look at him. My heart feels destroyed.

I trusted Callum and loved him fiercely, and he did this to me. It feels like a horrible nightmare I need to wake up from. I don't know what to do or where to go. I just know I need to get as far away from him as possible.

***

I put my car in park and turned off the engine. Sitting here in the pouring rain I survey the apartment complex in front of me. I didn't intend to come here. I feel utterly distraught and what I think I need more than ever right now is my best friend.

I exit my car and dart across the dark parking lot, running for Fallon's apartment. It doesn't take long before I'm standing in front of his door, I raise my hand and knock a couple of times tentatively. A quiet, "Coming," is the reply to the knocking.

Fallon opens the door and does a head-to-toe sweep of me, taking in my drenched appearance, my red eyes from crying, and my hopeless expression. He quickly scoops me up into his arms and hugs me fiercely. We stayed in the embrace for several minutes. During our hug, he pulled me into the apartment and locked the door.

He finally releases me, grabbing my shoulders and he gives me a very concerned look. "What is wrong, Fin?" I can't help it but when I see the concern from my best friend I break down without any embarrassment. I tell him everything. I finished talking a few minutes ago and Fallon hasn't said anything.

Why hasn't he responded? He just sits there on his couch, elbows on his knees, fingers laced together, head down. I'm getting more nervous the longer the silence continues. This isn't like Fallon to be so calm and quiet. I don't understand what is happening.

Finally, Fallon looks up. His gaze looks murderous. While I knew he would be mad at his brother for hurting me, I didn't expect this look of utter rage, and I didn't expect him to direct that look at me. Why is he looking at me like this? Shouldn't this anger be directed at Callum?

"Why are you here Fin?"

"I didn't know what to do and I just really needed my best friend right now Fal."

"So, what, you thought you would come here, and I would make you feel better? I would patch you up like I've done our whole lives. You would get comfort from me and then pretend I'm nothing just like always?"

My head rears back like I've been slapped. Why is he saying these things? He's my best friend. He is supposed to be who I call on when I am down. He is supposed to care that I am hurting. Why does he think he is nothing?

"Fallon, you're my best friend. You are not nothing. I don't understand. Why are you mad at me?"

He chuckles but it doesn't sound amused, it sounds evil. Like a villain in a movie who is about to destroy the heroine. He looks at me with cruel amusement in his gaze. "Get out, Finley."

"What?" I can't believe he just said that, why does he want me to leave?

"You heard what I said. Leave!"

"Fallon, why are you kicking me out? Why are you acting so terrible to me?"

"You are a slut who spread her legs for the wrong brother, Finley. You got what you deserved. He screwed you and then screwed you over. It was always going to end this way from the moment you picked him over me. Now your heart feels the way mine has for over a year. You broke my heart Finley; it's only fitting that Callum broke yours. Now get out. I'm done with you."

At his cruel words, I felt my heart crack. My chest felt heavy, and it was hard to breathe. How could my best friend, closest confidant, not only say these things but also truly feel them? Have I so badly misjudged him our whole lives? I couldn't meet his stare. I couldn't even move.

When it became clear I wasn't making my way to leave, Fallon picked me up, opened his door, dropped me on the concrete, and slammed the door in my face.

I was immobile, stunned at what happened. How could my perfect life implode so extremely? How did I have my heart broken twice in one night? How could everything of importance be taken from me so thoroughly when I had done nothing wrong?

It took a while to be able to get up and head to my car. It was still pouring rain like a monsoon, but I didn't even care as I was drenched. I didn't run or walk quickly to my car. I moved at the pace of a snail unable to fully wrap my head around my night.

As I started my car to head home, the only thought on my mind was that the MacGregor boys were dead to me.

FINLEY

It's been a long day but instead of being tired, I feel invigorated. I have only been on a handful of dates since Callum and I split up, and most of those never got a repeat. In my experience, I'm better off alone. But for some reason, I am excited about my date tonight.

When I had been out with Kai, I set up a date with someone on that Mate Match app. It was on a whim, as a way to feel better about myself and try to rid myself of the pain of seeing the MacGregor boys. I thought I set up the date with a hot vampire, but I must have been drunker than I thought. Tonight, my date is with a very attractive man—a *warlock*—named Alexander.

Ordinarily, I don't think I would have gone out with a warlock—I've never even met one—but I already set this up and what's the worst that can happen? I don't know much about warlocks; I've heard they perform dark magic and that's the difference between mages and witches. I guess I will find out for myself soon enough.

He didn't say what exactly we would be doing tonight just to dress in something I could comfortably walk in and that we would be spending the evening outdoors. It isn't a bad day for it. The weather is very temperate. Not too hot and not too cold. Sunny with a little bit of cloud cover, but no threats of rain or storms.

I stand in front of the mirror surveying my handiwork. I decided to wear my favorite jeans, they hug in all the right places but are also forgiving on the waistline and have rips on the knees. A burgundy peplum top makes my boobs look awesome. On my feet, I have a pair of black tennis shoes. I did a mostly natural look for my face makeup but did an on-point winged eyeliner in black. My long brown hair I have tied back in two Dutch braids. I was feeling pretty proud of the look I pulled off—casual, comfortable, and cute.

The doorbell rings and I check the clock, it's 7 p.m. exactly the time Alexander told me he would be here. Hey, he is very punctual, that's a good start.

I open the door and step out. I'm completely taken off guard by what I'm met with. The man in front of me is way more attractive than he looked in the photo on his dating profile. He is probably six foot tall, muscular, tan, with wavy brown hair, and eyes that look like honey. He is wearing all black—black ripped jeans, black V-neck, and black shoes. Both arms have several tattoos each. He looks like a dark god personified. What is this hot man doing going on a date with me? I feel like I'm being punked. Surely someone is pulling one over on me.

I take a deep swallow, then meet his eyes. "Um, are you Alexander Moretti?"

"Hello love, yes I am Alexander, you can call me Xan."

He smiles at me and holds eye contact. It feels like drowning to look into his eyes, like there is no escape but you would happily go to your death. His smile is a little lopsided, one side doesn't quite reach as high as the other, and for some reason, the quirk feels even more endearing.

I smiled back and realized I'd probably been looking at him too long, I probably looked creepy, and he was probably already regretting agreeing to a date with me. I look back toward my front door and lock it. Take a couple of steps toward him and say, "It's nice to meet you."

He sticks out his hand. We are going to shake hands. I don't think I've ever had a date start with a handshake before and this is probably a bad omen for how this night is going to go. I stick my hand out. He surprises me, instead of shaking my hand, he wraps his fingers around my palm and slowly drags my hand to his mouth. He kisses the back of my hand and lingers there for a moment. He releases my hand and drawls, "You are just as stunning as your photos." Then he follows that up with that fantastically lopsided grin. Swoon.

It was still light outside when we got into the car, but it was close to sunset. He told me the place he wanted to take me was a little bit of a drive but when we got into his black SUV it seemed like the thirty-minute drive passed quickly from enjoying our entertaining conversation. We turned onto an unmarked dirt road. The sun had already set and the area we are currently in is pretty dark. He comes to a stop in a field and turns the car off. With the car headlights no longer on the entire field is pitch black.

He got out of the car and is digging around in the trunk. I was completely at ease when I left my house but honestly, now I'm thinking maybe I made a grave error. I don't know this man and I got in his car. I let him take me to an undisclosed location. My cell phone doesn't show any signal. *Shit*. For all I know, Xan might be a serial killer who is going to murder me out here in the middle of nowhere and bury my body in this field. I'm such an idiot and I'm regretting my life choices.

Xan found whatever he was looking for in the trunk and came around to my side of the car. It's probably murder supplies. I just sat here waiting like a dummy while he was getting his gear to murder me.

When I make no move to get out, he grips the door handle and opens my door for me. His face is a mask of confusion and in his hand, he is holding two flashlights. "Is something wrong Finley?"

Flashlights. He was digging around in the trunk for flashlights—NOT murder weapons. I don't know whether to facepalm or praise the lord. Just as that thought leaves me, I realize, it might be too early to give thanks, maybe he is a murderer and already has his supplies where he intends to take me.

When my quietness goes on for probably too long. Xan reaches in, unbuckles me, and tugs my hand. He clicks on both of the flashlights and puts one in my free hand. Still unsure of what to do I look from the flashlight I'm holding to our joined hands, and then finally stop on Xan's face.

Seeming to realize the problem he says, "Oh. I'm sorry I didn't think about how this might look. Taking a beautiful woman out to the middle of nowhere after dark for a date."

He gives me a sheepish smile. It looks like an apology and a plea all at once. He turns me toward him and places his hands on my shoulders. He exhales a deep breath while looking at me then says, "I promise there is nothing untoward going to happen here. I wanted to show you my favorite place." He almost looks crestfallen at the idea that he did something wrong.

"This field is your favorite place?" I ask as I look around seeing nothing of particular interest. It is just an empty lot of land. The grass is overgrown and nothing visible that would lead me to believe it could be anyone's favorite anything.

He chuckles before he replies to my question, "No not this field. There is a waterfall a short hike from here that is my favorite place. You wouldn't be able to tell by looking around this place, but it is not far. I used to go there as a kid, I grew up not far from here. That is where I'm taking you. If you'll still let me."

A waterfall, he just wanted to show me a waterfall *not* kill me. Now I feel kind of like a big asshole. At this point I'm not sure if I'll be able to turn this around and salvage this—but I don't like seeing the frown marring his beautiful face either. I nod and gesture for him to lead the way.

We walked through the field for about ten minutes and now stand in front of a giant dark hole. According to Xan, it's a cave.

"We just have to walk through this cave and the waterfall is on the other side."

A dark spooky cave. *Lord, please help me, I'm too young to die, I'm only 23!* I should have trusted my gut earlier and made him take me back home.

Starting to back away slowly, keeping my eyes on Xan, I yell, "I don't think this is a great idea!"

After a few steps back, I turn and sprint back toward the direction of the car, not to get into the car obviously, but so I can find the direction back to the road. Before I can get more than five feet strong arms wrap around me and lift me, bringing me to an abrupt halt. Oh no! This is it. I'll never escape now.

"Shh. Calm down, love. I promise everything is okay. I'm being honest with you. The waterfall is just on the other side of the cave. The cave itself is also not inhabited by any creatures. I came here earlier today to set up for our date, so I know it is undisturbed."

I'm quietly panicking. I don't know a way to get out of this. I could try to fight him but is it worth it? He is much bigger than me, and he is a warlock. Warlocks have magical abilities. I have no earthly idea what those abilities are but surely, they would be handy in a fight. I contemplate my options for a minute, but I start to feel calmer and more relaxed without cause.

"If the cave is the issue that is causing you to be afraid, I can carry you to the other side. You could close your eyes; it would only be a couple minutes walk."

I look into Xan's face and see the sincerity in his eyes. It's probably against better judgment but for some reason, I feel like I can trust him.

"Okay." I give him a little nod and he walks us into the cave.

"Just hold on tight. Close your eyes, if you would like. I've got you, Finley."

I follow this advice and close my eyes. I hold tight to him and rest my head on his shoulder. He is so warm. I'm pleasantly surprised that he is so comfortable to rest against, which is something I wasn't quite expecting since I figured his muscular physique would be harder.

Xan walks us forward while simultaneously rubbing small circles on my back. It has a very calming effect on me. How did I go from being frightened to completely relaxed and trusting? I should probably be worried about that, but I can't find it in myself to care at the moment.

Before long he comes to a stop. I can hear the quiet roaring of rushing water. He slid me down his body to put me on my feet, my body came into contact with his body in quite a few places as he did so, and it sent my heart racing. "Open your eyes, Finley," he quietly whispers and turns me around.

I open my eyes and am completely awestruck by the sight in front of me. There is a small waterfall about ten feet away. Mist from the fall is spraying in the air around it but it is far enough away that it isn't reaching us. On the bank near the water is a flannel blanket spread on the ground. There is a Bluetooth speaker somewhere playing soft soothing instrumental music. Twinkling fairy lights are strung up on a couple of tree branches that hang above the blanket and on it sits a basket along with a bucket of ice with a bottle of strawberry-flavored wine.

I feel like such a jerk now for my earlier reaction to coming here and the situation involving the cave. This man is not only stupefyingly attractive but also so sweet to put this together and I acted suspicious and tried to run away! Not going to get a second date out of this one. Maybe I can still at least make him hate me a little less by the end of the night.

I turn around to face Xan, "This is stunning. I can't believe you did all this for me." I look down at my feet and push a pebble with the toe of my sneaker, feeling more than a little embarrassed. "I'm sorry about earlier."

He chuckles. "All is forgiven. I hope I didn't give off creeper vibes bringing you here." He gives me a questioning glance with one eyebrow slightly arched up, patiently awaiting an answer.

My whole face is flaming now. I feel so embarrassed that I thought badly of his intentions. "I might have thought you brought me here to murder me," I admit to my chagrin.

"Oh! That's why you tried to run! It wasn't being afraid of the cave. You thought I was an ax murderer." He releases a bellowing laugh.

"I'm sorry." I give a timid smile in apology.

He crosses his heart, "I promise, on my honor as a warlock, I've never killed not even one person." Then he gives me a huge grin. "Now come on, I packed us some treats."

With the air cleared and all forgiven, he grabs my hand and tugs me toward the picnic he assembled for us surrounded by the beautiful view and ambiance.

Five

Xan

Planning this whole evening out was extremely difficult for me—how does a commitment-phobe get the idea he can suddenly change his stripes? Maybe I'm in over my head. I've always made minimal effort with females in the past. I put in enough work to pique their interest but kept enough of myself locked away that I remained a mysterious guy they chose to only spend an evening with.

My go-to method for the past few years has been relying on women hitting on me at my nightclub and it occasionally leads to them coming upstairs with me to my apartment above the club. We would both have a good time and that was the end of it.

Despite my history, that is not what I desire with Finley. The moment I saw her I felt enthralled. I was under her spell, and she was none the wiser. I knew the moment I heard her setting up a date with another man that I would intervene. Some might say I played dirty by using magic to hijack the message from her intended recipient, but I knew she would be someone worth being the villain for.

I was out of my depth planning the date, so I relied on my best friends to help me. Hadeon, Ry, and Alder assisted me with decorating my favorite spot by the falls while Ry's mate Leora helped me plan and put together our picnic dinner. I think the teamwork pulled this off. From the moment she saw the setup she seemed happy.

I sit down on the blanket and pull her down with me. I desperately want to bracket my thighs around hers and snuggle close while we eat and enjoy each other's company, but I know I need to play this cool because she already showed signs of being skittish. I don't want to scare her away. I talk myself from the edge of coming on too strong and settle in close to her instead. Opening the picnic basket, I pull out two stemless wine glasses and set them on a fancy stone slab I brought to use as a makeshift table. Then I proceeded to pull out the meal I prepared. Leora recommended something referred to as 'girl dinner'. When she first suggested it, I had no idea what she meant, but after some research on the internet, I found it meant a charcuterie board. As I survey my efforts, I dare say I put together a good spread.

"Wow, this looks lovely." She says while taking inventory of the array of meats, cheeses, nuts, crackers, and fruits I included.

"I'm not familiar yet with what you like eating so I wanted to be able to give you lots of options. I might have overdone it;

we probably didn't need five different cheese choices." I say as I point out the section of the tray that contains the cheeses.

I must have done something right because she smiled at my confession. Handing her a plate from the basket we both set to work filling our plates. She picked a few of the cheeses, salami, crackers, grapes, and some pistachios. I fill both of our wine glasses with the chilled wine.

"So, this is my first time going out with someone from a dating app," she says. Then follows it up with, "Do you frequently use Mate Match?"

I already know this information from listening to her at the club, but I have to pretend to be oblivious to it. I look her in the eyes and say, "No. This is my first time using Mate Match." Not a lie, but I am not about to admit the only reason I have the app is because I heard her setting up a date and like a creep decided to intervene. Even to myself, it sounds a little predatory, not normally my style, but I can only imagine what she would think if she knew. I'll keep this information under lock and key.

I feel a smug satisfaction of being the first one to take her out on a date from one of these apps, I know it is unfounded seeing as I snatched her actual intended but what can I say? It is a highly enjoyable feeling. She doesn't know it, but I plan to be the last man she gets to know romantically. The moment I saw her I felt this instant pull toward her. I feel it deep in the marrow of my bones that she is meant to be mine. I've always laughed at people who believed in love at first sight and while I know this isn't love *yet*, I can see myself spending all my time with her.

Pulling my phone from my pocket I change the song playing on the Bluetooth speaker. I put on a sensual romantic song that we can slow dance to. I stand up and offer her my hand. "Will you dance with me?" I give her a smile that is hopeful but reserved because I'm nervous she will reject my proffered hand and offer to dance. But she surprises me by wrapping her hand in mine and letting me tug her up.

I adjust the hand I'm holding to be in the proper position for dancing, her other hand placed on my shoulder, and I place my other hand on the small of her back. We talk quietly while I sway her around in the clearing. My body is reveling at the feel of her pressed close. Nothing in my life has ever felt this right. It feels like she always should have been here. My soul feels calm and excited all at the same time, a total contradiction, but it feels perfect in this instance.

We danced to several songs. The closeness has been enjoyable, but I can tell she is starting to tire. I lead the way back to the blanket and this time I don't hesitate to position us close to each other. When we sit, I position myself in a way that wraps my body around hers. She doesn't seem to mind and snuggles close to my chest. It makes me wonder if she also feels this need to be close to me as well.

We talked for quite a while, snuggled close, with an additional blanket tucked around us, keeping us warm and cozy. My mind started to feel distressed by the idea of this night ending. What if when she left, I never saw her again? Would she go home and forget me? Unimaginable and irrational fear takes over. It wasn't my best idea, but a plan formed that calmed my harried nerves.

Silently I mouthed a quick charm to put her into a slumber. It wouldn't hold her longer than if she naturally fell asleep, but it would let me keep her in my arms while she rested.

Is it wrong to keep her here without permission? Maybe—well probably. But if I'm being honest there isn't much I wouldn't do to hold on to this moment. I wrap my arms securely around her and release a sigh of contentment when I breathe in the scent of her hair. Shortly after sleep finds me as well.

Six

FINLEY

Last night's date with Xan was meant to be an experiment for me, testing the waters of online dating. Loads of people I know have tried it, and the outcomes have been mixed, some love it and some hate it. I didn't have high expectations, but he exceeded any expectations I could have made. As embarrassing as it is to admit, I somehow fell asleep and snuggled up to Xan on our date. I couldn't believe that happened. I've never fallen asleep on a date before unless it ended at someone's house.

When I awoke and realized what I had done I was so worried I ruined the night we had. When I awoke, I was worried that he would be gone, or if he was still there, he would be angry. Those assumptions couldn't have been further from the truth. When I woke up and went to sit up, he was lying on the blanket watching me, looking at me with what appeared to be admiration. His watchful gaze made me feel beautiful, something I haven't felt too often lately.

After our date extended from a simple evening to an accidental overnight sleepover, I figured once we gathered up all our belongings we would go our separate ways, but he surprised me with wanting to continue our time together. We ended up going to a diner not far away and having a late breakfast together. After we stopped by his place to drop off the supplies from the previous night. He owns the nightclub I went to with Kai on the night of Angus MacGregor's funeral, and he lives in a loft above the club.

His place was surprisingly cozy. I don't know what I expected from a warlock but I kind of pictured a dark sinister environment based on the things I've heard about warlocks, but it wasn't like that at all. The loft was mostly open-concept. Hardwood floors in a blonde wood ran the expanse of the place. The kitchen featured green cabinets with gold pulls and stainless-steel appliances. His place was beautifully decorated and even had a large formal dining table that had seats for twelve. I asked about the large table, and he said he has a group of friends who are like family to him, they often come to his place to spend time together. He even said he would like me to meet them sometime and that I'd fit in well with them.

After he put all the belongings away, I spied around his two-bedroom apartment before we went to the downtown area for a little while. We took a stroll in the gardens there and also sat and talked for a while in the gazebo. We had such a great time together and it felt right, I never wanted it to come to an end, but sadly a message had been sent out to the pack requesting everyone's presence tonight for a mandatory meeting.

So here I am climbing into Kai's SUV on the way to whatever fresh hell the pack has going on now. I wish they would stop sending out mandatory meeting requests, some of us have a life or at least a lack of desire to be around everyone in the pack.

"What do you think it's about?" Kai huffs while heading toward our destination.

"No clue, but I'd be fine with being left out of it."

Within a few minutes, we arrived at the MacGregor household which is where the meeting will be today. Walking up to the house we see a sign on the porch directing all arrivals to go to the backyard. We walk around the house and reach the backyard which looks like a scene from a large family reunion-style barbeque. It looks like the majority of the pack arrived before us. There are a couple of the guys huddled around the grill, flipping burgers and hotdogs. Kids are playing yard games off to the side. They brought down a ton of tables and chairs like this was some big event rather than just a simple meeting. A sad thought hits me when I look at the tables and wonder if any of these are the ones that were purchased for the wedding reception for Callum and me. Our wedding was only a few months away at the time of our breakup and our ceremony and reception were to take place here at his parents' house. I'm annoyed at myself for evening thinking about it. No longer will I let him, and our past haunt me. I will not allow him to ruin my happiness.

I stalk over to a table and try to release the scowl from my face. Kai comes and takes a seat beside me, solidarity and all that. She strikes up a conversation with a couple of the older pack members that are at our table, I have no clue what they are talking about since I tune them out and try to think of when I might get to see Xan again. When we separated earlier, he was adamant about wanting to see me again. Not having experience with online dating, I didn't know how all this worked. According to Kai, most guys usually wait a couple of days to make contact again— if they contact you at all. She seemed to think that him already telling me he intended to see me again was a good sign and that he was most likely interested in a relationship rather than a fling. She told me a lot of people she's met from apps aren't like that. Thinking of seeing Xan makes me feel all warm and bubbly inside, if I feel like this after one night with minimal physical contact what would it feel like to have more with him?

Someone lets off a loud horn and everyone in the yard goes quiet. Rowan approaches the steps of the back porch where her three sons are currently standing. Once she climbs up to the porch, she looks around the group of us all and gives a small smile and a wave.

"Thank you all for coming on short notice. We planned to wait until the full moon to appoint a new alpha but unfortunately, there have been some issues that need to be addressed and cannot wait. Therefore, we will appoint the new alpha this evening so that whoever is chosen can start the process of getting control of the current issues of our pack."

Both Kai and I give each other looks of surprise with wide eyes. This is unprecedented to announce a successor at a time that is not a full moon pack meeting. As far as I know, this hasn't happened before. What could be going on with the pack that needs to be addressed? What issue can the former matriarch not handle on her own?

We don't get long to consider the possible reasons for the alpha pronouncement being moved up because after just a moment Rowan gestures to the back of the yard. Everyone turns in that direction to see a circle set up. I've never seen an alpha challenge before, but I've heard about them. Anyone interested in becoming alpha must fight in the ring. The goal isn't to kill or forever maim your opponents, but it occasionally happens.

All the MacGregor boys descend the porch stairs and start stomping over toward the challenge circle. Fallon looks confident, walking with his shoulders up and head held high. Callum looks resigned, but comfortable, almost like he doesn't want to go in but knows he must. Knox trails behind them taking his sweet time, the scowl on his face looks as if he is disgusted by the whole thing.

"If anyone else would like the chance to become alpha now would be the time to step forward. Once the challenge starts there can be no new additions," Rowan projects loudly to the crowd.

Most of the people in the crowd are shaking their heads in dismissal, none want to tempt the wrath of the longest-lasting line of alphas. I can understand their hesitation, I wouldn't want to fight any of their family either.

Once it is clear no one plans to step forward Rowan turns toward her boys, "Shift."

Callum and Fallon start stripping off their clothing and shifting into their wolf forms. Knox stands there with his arms crossed hesitating for a couple of minutes before his mother says, "Boy you better shift, you do not have a choice in this. As an heir of the former alpha, it is required that you at least make an attempt at the succession or else it is a great offense." If possible, Knox's scowl gets even deeper and he follows the same pattern as his brothers, stripping his clothing off and then shifting into his wolf form. All three stand around the circle waiting to be told when to enter and start the process.

Rowan nods her head, assessing her boys. Tears are starting to glisten in her eyes. She is trying to be strong in front of the pack, but I can tell she's full of nerves. I don't blame her, all her babies are going to get into that circle, and who knows if there will be any permanent injuries or deaths following the match. Despite my feelings toward the MacGregor boys, I wouldn't wish any of them dead. I'm even a little nervous about their fight.

"Okay. Now that you are already. You all will go into the circle. There will be a whistle to indicate it is time to fight. The winner will be named the alpha predecessor. Step forward now."

All three wolves prowl into the circle. All three have different colors of fur, similar to how they all have different colors of hair, which will make it easier to tell what is happening in the ring. Callum who has black hair also has black fur in his wolf form. Fallon has red fur, it is not the same color as his hair but still red. Knox, who is blonde, has white fur when in wolf form.

Knox sits down in the circle. His wolf form looks indifferent to his circumstances. Meanwhile, both Callum and Fallon are pacing back and forth, surveying each other, and both start growling, it starts as a rumble at first and changes to snarls rather quickly. I don't doubt that the winner is going to be either Callum or Fallon. Knox doesn't appear to care one way or the other about being alpha, he is just doing what is required of him. Callum's wolf form is bigger and stronger than Fallon's, but Fallon has always been more strategic and better at one-upping his brother in mental prowess.

After a few minutes of their posturing—the wolf equivalent of a dick-measuring contest if we are being honest—the whistle finally pierces through the noise. Surprisingly it isn't red or black fur that is seen pouncing first. White fur is streaking across the ring and collides with the others. Knox runs at his brothers, but right before reaching them, he turns his body, throwing his body into Callum's while his jaws reach out and bite Fallon who is standing nearby. I didn't think Knox had it in him to be the first to strike, it's obvious everyone else is just as shocked. His brothers jerk away from him. Fallon has blood dripping from his neck where Knox bit him. It isn't a ton of blood, but it still means Knox was the first to draw blood. Callum picks himself up off the ground and his snarls intensify.

Knox pissed both of them off now. Both ignore each other and start slinking across the circle toward where Knox ran after his attack. Both growling and approaching Knox like he was their prey, no longer the predator he had shown himself as. While they are approaching, Knox starts nervous pacing, frantically stepping paw to paw as if searching for a way out of the impending doom.

When Callum and Fallon both are standing in front of Knox they are visibly vibrating with unrestrained rage. You can see them shaking as they growl and snarl at him. There is nowhere for Knox to go. He will have to take them both on at once if he wants to continue. Earlier he had the advantage of a sneak attack on them, taking them by surprise, but now he is backed up to the edge of the circle where he cannot get further away.

Realizing if he takes them both on, he won't succeed, Knox does what is probably his only option. He lowers his body to the ground, pressing his nose to the dirt. It is a sign of submission, showing deference to others as a signal of his withdrawal from the challenge.

A whistle causes everyone to halt their movements as Knox is ushered from the circle. Once retreated he shifts back to his human form, and someone brings him some supplies to remove the mud so he can get his clothing back on. Once Knox is settled beside Rowan, a whistle again is blown to indicate it is time to resume fighting.

The fight seems to amplify aggression from both Callum and Fallon. Were they holding back when Knox was in the ring with them? I wouldn't put it past either of them to do that, they both always try to protect him the most, and it was clear earlier that Knox had no desire to be the alpha.

Both Callum and Fallon start strutting like caged animals. Both watch each other intently, deciding who will be the first to pounce. It doesn't take long before Callum charges top speed in Fallon's direction and even though Fallon has the advantage of being smaller and therefore more agile, he doesn't get a chance to dodge the attack. Callum tackled Fallon to the ground while on top of him with his jaws firmly clamped down on Fallon's neck. It looks like Cal decided to go for the same wound that Knox created earlier. Blood is starting to drip into a puddle on the ground. Panic is rising in me, and I feel my breath getting more strained. Fallon and I might not be friends anymore, but I still wouldn't want him to get badly injured.

Just when I think the fight is going to come to an end, Fallon flips Callum off of him. He flees to the other side of the circle, leaving a trail of blood behind. The bite looks terrible. Even if he can continue the fight there is concern about the amount of blood he's lost.

Fallon doesn't pace or attempt an attack. He is standing in place with one of his back paws repeatedly kicking at the dirt. What he's doing doesn't make sense to me and I think that's probably the case for most of us watching, however, I know Fallon better than most people, and I'm sure he has a reason for what he is doing, and it doesn't take long for us to find out.

Fallon raises his head to his brother in a challenge and stays put. Callum takes that challenge and runs at him at top speed. This time Fallon is prepared for him to come at him. Callum jumps in the air in an attempt to throw himself on top of his brother again but before he can Fallon dives to the side. Callum lands hard on the ground, his front right paw goes directly into the little hole Fallon dug. There is a loud *snap* noise, and it is followed by one of the most gut-wrenching howls I have ever heard. That horrifying noise is coming from Callum who still hasn't gotten off the ground. There is a bone sticking out of his leg above where his paw is connected.

Fallon stalks toward his brother still on the ground, his head lowered, a viscous look on his face. I'm a little nervous to see what happens next as I watch the calculated approach. Teeth bared, a loud growl from his mouth he got his brother's neck in his jaws and just continued holding his mouth there but not clamping down. This could be a death blow if he wanted it to be. There isn't time for Fallon to take further action against Cal because Callum lowers his head to the ground the same way that Knox did.

A loud whistle is released indicating the match is over. Falling backed away from Callum then threw his head back and let out a triumphant howl. It is followed by dozens of other howls as more members of the pack celebrate his win.

Callum got left behind while the win was being enjoyed. No one is moving toward him, and I know something needs to happen fast to his leg or it will have a bad effect on the healing process. I go back and forth about it but eventually give in and rush over to help him. I pet his head to try and calm down his sad wolf whimpers before moving to the injury. I grab his leg and with as much force as I can push the bone back in. It isn't a pretty way to deal with the broken bone, but it works in an emergency like this. The howls of pain he released when I snapped it back into place made my stomach twist and I felt like I was going to throw up. Luckily, I held it in.

Once his leg was addressed, Callum changed back to his human form. He was lying on the ground still naked in his puddle of blood. I walked over to the sideline and got a towel and his clothing. I walked back to him and while maintaining eye contact lowered to his level and set the items in front of him. Does he deserve my help? Probably not, but I am trying to be a bigger person. I've been trying to put the heartbreak he caused behind me and move on with my life. This act of kindness for him takes me by surprise, but in the back of my mind, I wonder if it had to do with Xan. I enjoyed my time with him on my date, I have a feeling that there could be something there with him, and holding on to the past won't help me continue to move forward.

"Fallon MacGregor is now the new official alpha of Fang!" Someone shouts.

Before the fight I wasn't sure who I wanted to be our new leader, I knew it would be one of them even if someone else joined the challenge. But now I have a nagging feeling that it would have been better for it to have been any of the other boys.

Walking away I head toward the car to leave, with one last glance over my shoulder my eyes make contact with Callum who is still looking at me. Turning back around I link arms with Kai, and we flee into the night.

Seven

XAN

Two Weeks Later

Peering over my shoulder I get a glance of Finley laying silverware next to each of the plates on my dining room table. For the past two weeks since our date, we have seen each other every single day. I don't know what it is about her, but I feel this insistent pull toward her. I just want to be with her every day, and when we are together, I dread the minute we have to separate. Never in my life have I felt like this, and it has me wondering if I'm losing my mind.

Whether it is logical or not I'm crazy for her, against all reason I feel myself falling hard for her. Tonight, I decided it is time to introduce her to my friends because they're my family and she is starting to own my heart. I want to merge the two and intertwine them so intensely that they can never unravel. I want her to be threaded to me, in all the ways, for always.

After discussing it with her we decided to host a dinner at my loft. We just got back from picking up some supplies at the grocery store and while I'm performing the cooking duties, Finley is helping prepare the table. She has been trying to hide it from me, but I can tell she is nervous. She thinks I can't tell but in reality, I can read her like a book. There is no reason for her to be nervous though. I know my friends, will love her, and if she wasn't the wonderful person she is, they would at least make an effort because she is mine. *Mine.* The thought is echoing in my head. Is she mine? We haven't discussed anything in-depth and haven't put any labels on anything. Yet we have been spending all our free time together. What if she doesn't feel the same way as me? What if I am in too deep and I'm just a passing amusement for her? Suddenly this train of thought has me feeling sick to my stomach. We need to have a serious discussion soon to address this.

Knock. Knock.

I turn to the source of the noise just in time to see the front door open. Two of my best friends walk in, Hadeon and Alder. Hadeon is one of the only vampires I've ever liked. I can't stand most of the species, but he is a good guy and like a brother to me. Alder is a giant of a man, well technically, a giant of a squatch. Most squatches are antisocial and prefer to live a solitary existence in the wilderness, only coming into society to find a mate, then retreating to the woods. Alder, while looking like your typical squatch, lives in town, hangs out with us, and is generally an outgoing guy.

"Hey!" Alder bellows with a chin lift in my direction.

Walking towards me Alder gives a typical frat boy-style handshake. Hadeon, on the other hand, just gives me a nod. We are super close, but Hadeon is probably the more introverted of our group. A lot of his backstory is a mystery to us. We know he is a couple of hundred years old, he won't give us an exact age or tell us his birthdate, but he only appears to be the equivalent of a human male in his mid-thirties. He is originally from Eastern European descent, and despite moving away from there quite a long time ago, he still has an accent. We have asked a few times where he originated from, but he always finds a way to brush off our questions or deflect to a different topic.

After introducing them all to Finley I went back to my preparation duties in the kitchen. Hadeon followed me to the kitchen and perched on the counter opposite me. Alder on the other hand stayed with Finley. Glancing back toward the dining area, it appears they are becoming fast friends, they are laughing together as Alder helps her with setting the table.

"So, this is the mystery woman, huh?" Hadeon asks while eying her.

"Mystery no longer," I replied to him.

He takes several deep breaths, nostrils flaring on each inhale. I know what he's doing, and I'm not impressed by his antics.

"She's a shifter?" He asked me.

"Yes, I'm sure you can tell from that deep smell you just took. You creep."

"What type of shifter is she? Does she have a pack association or is she a loner?"

It feels a little irritating that he is asking me so many questions about my girl. Bro is too nosy for his own business. I want them all to like her and get to know her, but I don't see why all of this matters. Despite the annoyance of the situation, I answered him, "She is a wolf shifter. She is part of the Fang pack."

There is a second where a look of what I think is intrigue flashes across his features, but in a moment, it is gone. Bringing his arms up, he crosses them over his chest. He just sits there assessing me and deep in thought before finally saying, "And how do they feel about one of their own seeing someone outside of the pack? Someone non-shifter."

My irritation flared higher with the questions he asked. I honestly don't know the answer to either question.

"We haven't discussed it. She doesn't talk much about the pack. If I'm being honest it seems like there is some weird history there. She seems to spend less time with the pack than any shifter I've known."

He goes back to looking at Finley, it is making me feel a little uncomfortable. I feel like the wheels are turning in his head more than words are coming from him. There is something he isn't saying, I can tell.

"Fang is one of the toughest, largest packs. It is also one that usually does not tolerate dating or mating outside of shifters within the pack. You might want to ignore the elephant in the room, hiding behind your newfound happiness but you need to have a conversation about this. It could be putting a target on your back being with her."

He might be right, but it doesn't mean I have to like or believe it. The answer doesn't matter to me anyway. I am going to hold on to this girl, and no one is going to be able to take her away from me. That intense thought has my heart galloping in my chest.

"What's wrong? Why did your heart rate increase so much? You sound like someone who is in a panic." Hadeon narrows his eyes on me.

Maintaining eye contact with him, "No one is ever going to take her from me." I grind out, "I'll kill anyone who tries."

***

Once Ry and Leora arrived for the group dinner things settled in and Hadeon seemed to drop the earlier subject for the time being. Ry has been my friend for the longest out of any of our crew. We grew up together. We got along swimmingly even when we met despite what the world says about satyrs. Most say they have one of the biggest attitudes of all the different species of paranormals. While he can tend to be a bit of an asshole to others, he's always had my back. Not only is he my best friend but he also helps at my nightclub as one of the bartenders and helps with some of the management duties that my magic business sometimes distracts me from.

"So, I see you ended up with a date from that Mate Match app after all," Ry says to Finley with a cheeky grin. The bastard is well aware of what I did to get a date with her, but he has promised to keep my secret.

"Oh, have you met before?" Leora questions.

"Yep. Finley came into the nightclub one night a few weeks ago with a friend. I was on bartending duty that night. They were pretty tipsy if I remember correctly and her friend forced her to download Mate Match, it's a dating app for paranormals. Finley tried pretty hard to fight against it, but it seems like it worked out for her." Ry replied to his mate.

Leora, who is a light fairy, starts glowing. "That's wonderful."

"Yeah, to be honest, it was my first time using any type of online dating, as well as the first time I've gone out with anyone who wasn't pack. My best friend, Kai, the one who was with me at the club that night, is the one who pushed me to step out of my normal comfort zone. I haven't had the best luck in the past with relationships, so I haven't spent much of my time putting myself out there the past couple of years." Finley gives details to Leora.

Hadeon looks pointedly at me before turning his attention to Finley, "Does Fang prohibit relationships with outsiders? I know some packs are strict on the matter."

That dickhead just couldn't let that go, he had to bring it up. Her bringing up the fact that I'm the first she'd dated outside of the pack left him a perfect opportunity to bring it up.

She gets a nervous demeanor about her and starts slightly twisting her hands in front of her while resting them on the table. She glances at me making eye contact before turning back to Hadeon. "It isn't necessarily against the rules. Officially they have no rules in the books about it. I know because Kai has never dated anyone in the pack and has gone into detail about the lack of rules. But it is something that would most likely be frowned upon. As far as I know, the new alpha won't be changing that but he's unpredictable, so I don't know what'll happen."

She seemed to get a scowl when she brought up the new alpha, it piqued my curiosity. We never really discuss anything about the pack, so this is one of the first times I've heard anything about a new alpha. "What's the situation with the new alpha? Do you get along?" I ask.

She frowns deeply. "Not so much anymore. His name is Fallon. He used to be my best friend. Growing up we were inseparable." I feel a slight twinge of jealousy at her words, which is unfounded. "We have a history that has caused some bad blood between us as well as his family."

I really shouldn't care but I can't help but despite our current company I can't help but to ask, "Did you date him?"

Head down staring at the table, I start to wonder if I should have minded my own business when she looks back at me and has a glisten to her eyes. Tears aren't falling down her face, thankfully, but her eyes are starting to gather some.

"No, we didn't date. But his older brother and I were engaged at one point while I was in college. Our relationship ended when I caught him with another woman right in front of everyone at a college party. According to some of his frat brothers, she wasn't the only one. Everyone knew and no one told me due to their loyalty to him."

I feel a little bad now for asking, now that I know she went through something that probably broke her heart, but I can't help but continue asking for more information. I feel a strong need to know what happened. "I'm sorry, that's shitty. What happened with the alpha? Why don't you guys get along?'

"He was my best friend and when I was heartbroken and hurting, needing support from my best friend more than ever, he kicked me when I was down. I never realized but allegedly he had been in love with me for years. So, when I told him what happened he threw it in my face out of jealousy and made sure I knew it was my fault. He made sure I knew that he didn't have any sympathy for me. According to him, it was my fault because I chose his brother over him. I had never thought about him as anything other than a friend, practically a brother to me. So, I was completely taken off guard to find out that not only did he have feelings for me romantically but that he could say such cruel things to me as he did that night. He tossed me out in the rain, and we have barely spoken since then. Any conversations we have had since have only been out of the necessity of pack activity and even that I try to avoid."

Leora, who had been pretty quiet most of the night asked, "Do you think he's going to try to give you any trouble now that he is alpha? Like do you think he will try to get back at you for any perceived grievances?"

Finley nibbles on her lower lip in silent contemplation for a few minutes before responding. "I don't think so. But if he does, as lame as it might sound, I'll go to his mom about it. She was practically my second mom growing up and she loves me. Plus, she was devastated about what happened with her oldest son, even though it was not her fault. Fallon is a big momma's boy and he hates displeasing her, he'll do practically anything to stay on her good side."

***

The night went along pretty well. To my pleasure, everyone seemed to like Finley. There was no doubt Alder, our extrovert of the group, or Leora, our sweetest member, would love her. Ry already met her and seemed to get along just fine with her last time so that friendship only compounded when they spent time together this evening. Hadeon, he's the one I was the most nervous about, but he seemed okay with her, mostly his discontentment was with the idea of her pack not accepting us as being in a relationship due to a lot of shifter species keeping relations within their species—more specifically within the pack.

We had a delicious homemade pasta dinner accompanied by a salad that Hadeon helped throw together. Afterward, we all had some wine and dessert that Ry and Leora grabbed at the market on their way here. It ended up being a really fun time.

Everyone except Finley recently departed to go home for the evening. She is still here, and she insisted on helping clean up from the dinner party. I tried to tell her not to worry about it, but she wouldn't take no for an answer.

After getting the trash taken down to the dumpster behind the club, I lock the door and look toward Finley. She is currently at the kitchen sink hand washing some of the dishes. Walking up behind her I wrap my arms snugly around her waist and rest my head on her shoulder.

"I told you that you didn't need to do that," I admonished her.

"I know, I know. I just didn't want to stick you with all the mess."

Turning my head slightly I run the tip of my nose along her skin from the crook of her neck to just behind her ear. With my mouth right near her ear, I quietly say the words to a spell. Once my words are complete all the dishes start washing and assembling in their proper locations.

She chuckles at my antics, and I grip her waist tighter, not ready to separate myself from her. "Will you stay the night tonight?" I whisper.

With my head tilted forward I slowly kissed her collarbone. Trailing kisses up her neck until I get close to her ear where I nibble on her lobe.

"Yes. I think I would enjoy staying the night." She says in a breathless voice.

Nothing more than kissing has transpired with us yet, but I am ready for more and I believe she is too. I've been craving her like a drug that I haven't even gotten to sample yet. Just the idea sends my heart racing.

"I wish I had known to pack an overnight bag though. I don't have any of my stuff with me."

"That won't be a problem, I can conjure some items for you." I give her a salacious smirk as I run my eyes over her body.

"I'm sure you can," she huffs with feigned displeasure.

While Finley used the master bathroom to take a shower, I took that as my cue to make some mood-setting preparations. My room, much like the rest of the house, has many candles lying about. It is something that kind of comes with the territory when you are a warlock or other magic caster. I snap my fingers simultaneously lighting all the candles in the room. None of them are scented, they are just for the warm glow. The Bluetooth speaker on my dresser is quietly playing some instrumental music that is very sensual.

Finley pokes her head out, shielding her body behind the bathroom door. Her cheeks are tinged a beautiful rosy pink. "Really Alexander? This is what you decided to conjure me for bed clothing?" Her tone showed more amusement than annoyance.

Shrugging my shoulders playfully I respond with, "I thought it would look beautiful on you, but you would also be beautiful without it." From the way her cheeks get more pink, I know she can feel the heat in my eyes as I watch her, waiting for her to stop hiding.

She makes a small huffing noise and then emerges from behind the door. The door slowly glides open as she stands in the doorway. It might not be playing fair, but I conjured her a black sheer lace babydoll nightie with a black thong for underwear. While I do like to use my magic to my advantage, an example being when I used magic to steal her date, I would never try to force something on her she wasn't ready for or wanting. The outfit was intentional to help her feel sexy but if she was uncomfortable, I would be happy to conjure anything else she wanted to wear even if it was a fuzzy one-piece that covered almost every inch of her flesh.

She takes a few steps toward me shyly, the candles exposing her to me. Words momentarily dry up in my throat as I drink in the sight of her. She looks magnificent. The sight of her has my blood rushing and my cock swelling. Her full breasts are covered by the black lace but with the sheer material, her pink nipples are visible. They look fucking perfect. The material of the top comes down only just past her hip level, if she were to turn, I'm sure I would get a pleasant view of her luscious ass.

Continuing toward me she only stops when she is a few feet in front of me. She has a small grin gracing her face. The mix of happiness and nervousness is evident.

"Are you comfortable with this? I can get you something else if you aren't."

"No, it's fine. I quite like it. It fits better than anything I've purchased for myself at the store."

I'm thankful that the outfit received her approval. She looks like a living goddess wearing it.

Two steps have me crowding close to her body. Tilting forward towards her face I tentatively place a kiss on her lips. She doesn't hesitate to deepen the kiss and slip her tongue into my mouth, slowly caressing my own.

Reaching around I grab her just below her ass cheeks and lift her. She wraps her legs around my waist as I carry her toward my bed. Never breaking the kiss, I situate myself on the edge of the bed while she straddles my hips.

"Love, you're fucking gorgeous. You took my breath away when I saw you in that outfit." I whisper with my mouth still almost touching hers.

She gets a twinkle in her eyes at my statement and then she lunges back to my lips, kissing me with more passion than before. My hands roam her body sliding up and down her back, then down to cup her ass, I run them down her thighs.

The feeling of warmth feels like it is penetrating my entire body continuing to ramp up my desire for her. Hands clutching her ass I start rocking her hips slowly but with force, thrusting her center against mine. A soft moan followed by a whimper escaped her after a few rocks. That damn whimper has me twitching in my jeans.

I wrap my arms around her waist and when I have her securely held to me, I toss us backward to drag us more fully onto the bed, before landing on my back, positioning her hips over my mouth.

"Xan, what're—," she cuts off with a groan when I push her underwear aside and using my tongue slowly start stroking her clit. Continuing to slowly caress her with my tongue, her body starts to slowly melt against me.

"That," gasp, "feels good." She says in between panting breaths.

Using two fingers I trail down to check her, when I feel her wetness, I hook them inside of her and work them in and out slowly while I continue the ministrations with my mouth.

Her muscles are starting to tighten, clenching and unclenching. Her release is hovering close. She does a small rock of her hips. "Sorry," she whispers.

"No, I want you to take your pleasure. Ride my face." I encourage her to keep going.

She bites her lower lip, not looking sure for a moment before she gives in and starts to rock rhythmically against my mouth. Her movements start methodical and paced, but it isn't long before her thrusts start being more erratic as she gets closer to bliss.

Her release hits and she lets out a moan and falls over me, as if her body just finished an intensive workout that left her boneless. I continue licking, sucking, and pumping through her throbbing aftershocks.

I place a kiss on the inside of her thigh. "Mm. You taste intoxicating."

Her face flushes with my admiration of her arousal.

She slides down my body and kisses me slowly and deeply. She clutches my shirt in one first and against my lips and says, "I want you. Now." A deep rumble of a chuckle releases from me at her demand. She just had a satisfying orgasm, but it only seemed to increase her desire. "I *need* you inside of me."

Damn. I was going to try and take this process slow but how can I deny her request? She said she needed me, and I desperately needed her too.

"There are too many layers." She says as she surveys my current state, still dressed in my clothing from the dinner party.

"Take these off." She practically growls the words at me while frantically trying to shred my clothes off of my body.

Pulling my shirt off I toss it onto the floor not caring where it lands. Next, my shoes, and then before I can take care of it myself, she grabs the button on my jeans and pops it open, followed by yanking my zipper down with force. She keeps her eyes locked on mine, licking her lips, she slowly drops to her knees at my feet. Reaching into my boxer briefs she springs out my erect cock.

Running her thumb over the head she collects a bead of precum, then slides her thumb into her mouth and sucks the liquid off. "Delicious," she purrs.

Using her tongue, she slowly licked my cock in a swirling motion. Then she wrapped one of her small soft hands around my base and started slowly pumping me. Her other hand comes up and cups my balls while gently kneading them. Just when I think things can't get any better, she parts her lips and wraps them around my tip before taking the upper portion into her mouth.

She starts sucking on me while also running her tongue gently around me, all while continuing to pump and knead. Nothing has ever felt this good in my entire twenty-seven years of existence.

A few minutes of her attention have only heightened my desire and need for her. This is great but I need to be inside of her with a frantic desperation.

Wrapping my hand around her ponytail, I give a small tug and her mouth comes loose from me with a slight *pop*. She looks at me confused for a moment, probably wondering if something is wrong. I don't give her the time to stress about it and with a deeply needy voice I tell her, "I need to fuck you right now. I need to be inside of your delicious cunt."

The small smirk that flashes across her features in acknowledgment sends shivers down my spine. She is so beautiful; I don't know how I got so lucky to be the bastard bringing her to my bed.

Tugging her up to standing I lowered my head and devoured her mouth with a kiss. Wrapping my arms around her waist I spin us around and lower her to the center of the mattress. I crawl up her frame and hover above her taking in her glorious body, it is a sight to behold. Sliding my hands slowly up her soft thighs I continue their upward path until I reach those black sexy panties. Sliding the palm of my hand against her center I discover something that feels like a coveted reward. "Mm, so wet for me. Your panties are soaked, Fin." Pulling the straps of her panties down I removed them from her body. Sliding my erection against her folds, it becomes coated in her arousal. "Do you want me to impale you with my cock and fuck you until you don't know your name?"

She doesn't answer me but starts squirming, trying to get friction by rubbing against me. I raise one eyebrow at her. She will get nothing from me until she gives me an answer, it is her choice after all. Picking up on the fact that I won't continue until she answers she breathlessly says, "Yes, Xan. Please don't make me wait any longer."

With her satisfying my question, I give no hesitation as I slide my cock through her folds, and push into her wet heat. After a few slow pumps in and out, I am fully sheathed inside her. We both sigh deeply with the pleasure of our connection.

Thrusting into her is like magic. There are tingles through-out my whole body, and it feels like something monumental is happening inside me, something life-changing. My senses feel heightened as I lose control, thrusting harder and faster into her. She consumes everything about me. Her hands ran down my spine, leaving light scratches. Her heavy breathing and soft moans drown out any outside noise. Her lips kissed mine, our tongues gliding against each other commingling the taste of arousal from both of us pleasuring each other earlier. My eyes greedily take in the view of where we connect as I continue to pump forward. The skin of her body is soft like the finest silk as I run my fingers across her chest. All five of my senses are consumed completely by her.

The need to be deeper steals over me. I grab her hips and never break our connection; I bring us up. I'm resting on my knees now with her straddling me. Able to get deeper now I continue my upward drive into her while she moves her hips to meet me thrust for thrust. Her beautiful breasts are now in my face as they bounce with every movement. I lean forward and pull a pink nipple into my mouth and suck. She releases a loud moan at the new feeling.

The sound of her moan broke something inside me. I felt a snap and the overwhelming feeling to *claim*. My movements become frenzied as I unleash on her. *Mine. She is mine.* These thoughts repeat in my head getting loud and louder. I desire nothing more than to fuck her until she knows there will never be another for her, to drive myself so deep that it leaves a mark on her soul. *Mine.*

Her pussy starts clamping on me, pulsing and fluttering. She is close to her orgasm and so am I. Flicking my tongue along her nipple a couple more times I pull my head away slowly making sure my teeth scrape her flesh. It sets her over the edge and the dam of her pleasure breaks free. Her movements get wilder and more uncontrolled, and I fuck her through it with my arms caging her to my chest. Her breathy moans near my ear are my undoing. My release hits me. As I spill into her, I feel a sense of the most blissful peace wash over me. I feel complete. I feel like my soul has been mended. It feels like something that I never knew was missing has been found and now I will treasure it for the rest of my life and even the afterlife.

We collapse onto the bed, and I wrap her in my arms to snuggle close. I didn't understand some of the things that were happening in my mind. Why was I so frantically insistent I needed to *claim* her? What even is that about? I've never once thought about that when with a woman. The possessiveness I felt over her didn't fade with completion, I still have the feeling I need to continue to torment her with my dick, filling her with so much come that it drips down her legs when she gets out of bed. The idea to make her continue to wear my pleasure is almost appealing. The thought of her wearing my scent and covered in my seed alerts anyone she comes into contact with that she is *mine and I am hers.* What the hell is wrong with me? These feelings are so outlandish and beyond any normal experience for me. My internal monologue with myself has me feeling like some possessive asshole.

My hand which is not tucked under her has been rubbing up and down her flesh. Only after I come out of my thoughts do I realize what I've been subconsciously doing, my hand has been rubbing back and forth along her lower stomach. Suddenly I feel panicked by what my action brought to mind, then the vision of her womb swollen with child flashes in my mind, and I have to say I don't quite mind the idea of planting my seed inside her. But this is all too fast, so I shake off the thought. "Are you on any form of pregnancy prevention?" I ask her.

She looks at me with a look of mild horror. "Uhm, no I'm not anything at the moment. It's, uh, been a while since I needed to." She flushes a little bit at the confession and looks away, biting her lip in nervousness. The cavity around my heart feels warm and internally I feel full of smug satisfaction that I am the only one she has been with in a while. She turns back toward me and says, "Don't worry, I'll stop by the pharmacy on my way home in the morning."

"That's okay, I have something you can take if you would like."

She gives a small head nod. We both got dressed, me into a pair of gray sweatpants sans shirt and her in some cute pajamas I conjured for her. Could I have conjured pajamas earlier instead of lingerie? Yes, I could have, but I had a feeling that things were going to get heated.

Eight

FINLEY

My emotions have been on such a rollercoaster tonight. At first, I was nervous because I knew I was meeting all the people important to Xan, he doesn't have any living family, so his circle of friends is his family. Then during the dinner when my old relationship failure came up, I was a little down, not for missing Callum, but for the pain I went through after our split and the loss it caused me of my best friend. After that uncomfortable truth came out the night got much better and honestly was a lot of fun. After everyone left the apartment, I was back to nervous when Xan asked me to stay the night with him. I've been wanting to stay but with us never having been intimate before I was excited but nervous with the idea of opening up to him in that way, despite wanting to. I was full of bliss so consuming it was like a high until Xan asked about contraceptives because then I realized in our fog of lust, we hadn't even discussed protection. I've never failed to keep myself before, I've always been on birth control and have always very adamantly insisted on condom use. All past sexual encounters I've participated in have been with protection. So, I had a combination of emotions about the fact we hadn't used a condom. I was slightly horrified at first because I didn't need to be getting impregnated by someone, I started dating only a few weeks ago, and there is so much we don't yet know about each other. But the other emotion I had trouble controlling was confusion, I have always used condoms, even with Callum who I was supposed to marry, but I felt comfortable enough with Xan that I didn't even worry about the idea.

If I'm being honest with myself, the panic was only momentary, and then I felt over it. What happened with Xan felt *right*. Deep in my soul, I felt like it should've always been him. I'm being silly, I shouldn't feel such a deep connection with someone I've only just recently met.

Xan leads me to his *office*. It isn't the office used for the club; it is where he does his magical work. He's told me before about the things he does for income besides the nightclub, but I've never seen his workspace for it. It's a large open room with metal tables spanning two of the walls. The wall across from the entryway has shelves covering the whole wall that is stuffed full of ingredients and supplies. Around the door we just walked through there are additional shelves filled with books, many I can recognize as grimoires which he must use for spellcasting.

"So, this is where the magic happens, huh?" I glance over my shoulder at him as I ask.

As he rummages around on the supply shelf, twisting small bottles to look at the labels, he replies, "Yes, Love, this is where I spend my time, doing projects for my real occupation."

He was very upfront with me about the magic business, including telling me some of the more unsavory spells some people request from him. He didn't have to tell me about any of this, but the fact that he was willing to let me in on his secrets warmed my heart. We had a lot of discussions afterward and agreed not to keep secrets from each other. It was his idea to be open and honest about everything with each other, it endeared me to him even more, especially with the betrayals I have suffered due to other people's secrets.

"Ah, here it is." He says as he snatches a small vial off the shelf and walks over to me. It is a very tiny container with just a small amount of purple liquid inside. I've not used anything like this before, but I haven't spent time with anyone who does magic before either, I've always just gone with traditional methods of birth control.

He presents me with the potion, and I pull the cork stopper from the top. I sniff the bottle, I was expecting it to smell foul for some reason, but it smells like cotton candy. "Do I just drink it?" I ask him curiously.

"Yes"

I tip the bottle toward my mouth and just chug it like I'm doing a shot at a bar. Again, my preconceived notion is that this would taste gross but I'm once again wrong, tastes the same as it smells. It's relieving that it wasn't something that would make me gag from the nasty taste, this went down easily.

"Mm. That was interesting. I wasn't expecting it to taste like cotton candy!" I exclaim to him with a smile.

"It's made to taste whatever flavor the drinker would enjoy most. It is an invention a witch came up with a couple of decades ago to make sure people weren't tossing it up from the disgusting taste. Trust me the previous method was truly unpalatable." He chuckled a little thinking about it.

"Alright, crisis managed. Let's get back upstairs so I can get you to bed. I won't be responsible for you being overtired tomorrow." With that said he ushers me back upstairs with a soft hand to my lower back.

Nine

XAN

I t's been a couple of hours since Finley and I came back to my bedroom to go to sleep for the night. Lying in bed, with her wrapped in my arms, holding her close while she is restfully sleeping has been a dream. I should be sleeping too but something is nagging at my brain, and I can't get it to turn off and join her in blissful slumber.

Unable to continue this anxious pattern of just lying here staring at the wall I decided to take matters into my own hands. I quietly slid out of bed and went to my bathroom closet. After a couple of minutes of digging I found what I was looking for, the sewing kit I keep for when I need to make small repairs to clothing. Opening the kit, I grab a sewing needle and take it to the sink to make sure it is clean. Once that is done, I walk back into the bedroom.

I creep over to Finley's side of the bed and lower to my knees. Her hands are tucked underneath her pillow, thankfully the fingertips are sticking out from underneath and accessible. After chanting a quiet spell to keep her from being disturbed from sleep I prick her finger with the needle and collect a couple of drops of blood.

Careful not to drop the sample I take it downstairs to my workspace. Something has been bugging the tar out of me all night and I intend to get answers. Having sex with Finley was the best experience of my entire life, but I've felt different ever since. The difference doesn't feel bad, it's just something I noticed, and I don't understand what it is that has changed within me.

At the bookshelf, I grab out the grimoire that has to do with blood magic and bring it to one of the tables. Sometimes blood can tell us stories that aren't written in words. Flipping through the pages I stop when I find the section I was hunting for. Placing a candle on the table I light the wick. On a piece of wax paper, I place a drop of her blood, the herbal ingredients needed for the spell, and then I cut myself and leak a drop of my blood onto it. Once it is all arranged on the paper, I crumple it up and hold it in the flame.

The flame of the candle went from its warm orange glow to a searing red and flared bright before returning to normal. The spell I chanted is complete and presumably successful based on the light change. Pulling the paper from the candle I pull it on the table to cool off enough to be able to handle.

Once the paper reaches a manageable temperature, I unfold it. The information on the paper is dumbfounding. Our blood samples match. I don't understand how our blood looks the same when we aren't even the same species, let alone who knows whether we have the same blood types. This leaves me more questions, so I go back to my book and start researching.

About an hour and three grimoires later I now understand. She is my mate. Fate-blessed mates are not very common anymore and only happen in about two percent of the paranormal community leaving most to take a chosen mate instead. No one in my family has had a fates-blessed mate as far as I'm aware, and I only have one pair of mated friends–Leora and Ry. Lack of knowing other mates left me lacking in knowledge surrounding them. It all makes sense to me now, why I felt such a primal drive to claim Fin, why I craved her, why my senses felt heightened with her, why my stupid mind kept screaming possessive thoughts over and over at me.

Something I can only describe as giddiness grabs hold of me. From the minute I saw Finley at my nightclub I've felt the need to do anything within my power to get close to her and make her mine. Now that I know she is my fates blessed mate, I realize two things, first I wasn't just acting like a crazy asshole stealing a date from a woman I'd never even talked to, and two she's mine and always will be.

The peace of learning and understanding what was happening within me has me feeling much more relaxed and finally feeling like I can rest easy. Deciding that I will clean up my mess at a more reasonable hour I leave behind my workspace and head back upstairs to my apartment.

When I get to my room, I find Finley still curled up in bed sleeping peacefully. I take a minute just to admire this gorgeous female that I get to spend all my time with. She is everything and I will keep nothing of myself guarded from her. She can have my body, heart, soul, my life. With that reverie, I slide quietly back into the bed, take a deep breath, and smell her hair as I tuck my head into the crook of her shoulder and neck before passing out for the night, finally.

Ten

FINLEY

A small amount of sunlight streaming into the room comes in between the curtain and the window. The sunlight falls across my face warming my skin. The feeling is pleasant, almost as pleasant as the sleep I got last night. Sleep has never felt so good in my life. Being wrapped up in Xan's arms felt safe and warm. He felt like coming home when you didn't even realize you never even had one, to begin with.

It is strange to think he feels like home to me, but I've only known him for a short time. We both have lived lives that the other knows nothing about, yet something shifted last night. What happened between us solidified something inside me and I know that he will be part of my story for the rest of my days. Never do I want to go back to being without him.

As I start to rouse more the smell of something delicious, scented wafts from outside the room. I stand up and do a good deep stretch, muscles I didn't even know I had been feeling sore today, can't say I mind it that much though, since I know what caused that soreness. Stretching completed, I stroll from the room to see where Xan is.

Out in the kitchen, I discover Xan, standing in the kitchen shirtless, cooking at the stove. He hasn't heard me approach yet, so I just take a minute to appreciate his morning appearance. His back muscles flex as he is stirring whatever it is he is cooking, and the sight is mouthwatering.

I'm walking closer, eyes never leaving his muscled butt when he must hear me, he turns around and I get caught in the act of checking him out. The way his lips pull into a smirk tells me everything I need to know at this moment, he knows exactly what I was doing. Busted! Hey, it's a great sight to see, I feel no embarrassment about it seeing as I got to see that sight completely naked last night.

"Morning, Love." He smiles and I think it's the first time I've seen a genuine smile from him, a real one that is pure happiness causing a few light crinkles to show next to his eyes. Happiness looks good on him, it makes my heart feel like it's doing flips in my chest, swooping low and then flinging back up. My lips automatically lift into a smile in return.

"There is a cup of coffee on the table for you." He gestures toward the table, and I see two mugs sitting there on top. "I'm just finishing up breakfast and was just about to come to wake you up, but I see you've beat me to surprise you with breakfast in bed." There is no disappointment in his tone of voice, thankfully.

The first sip of coffee hits my taste buds, and it is exquisite. An excellent, way to start the morning. "Do you need any help with any breakfast preparations?" I ask over my shoulder.

"Nah, I'm plating it up right now. Just take a seat and I'll be there in just a second."

There are a couple of clanking noises as he scoops whatever is in the pan and places it onto a plate. Once he has the food plated, he walks out holding both plates and approaches me with a big grin. He places a quick kiss on my cheek and sets a plate in front of me. He made us bacon, scrambled eggs, and some chopped fruit. It all smells and looks delicious. After just waking up I feel ravenously hungry and after a fast mumbled thank you I immediately dig into the food.

We eat breakfast alternating between talking and companionable silence. Sometimes silence can be bothersome or awkward, but I don't feel that way with Xan. I just get to soak up his presence and that makes me happier than any ideal small talk could.

As we are finishing up breakfast my phone buzzes several times and after checking the caller ID, I decided I better answer it. It is Rowan, which seems weird to me, I don't know why she would be calling me first thing in the morning. I raise my eyes to Xan and tell him, "Sorry I got to grab this really quick." I answer the phone but don't leave the table because I don't think anything Rowan would call about could be anything that I would need to deal with in private.

"Hi, Rowan," I say after hitting accept.

"Good morning, Finley. Hope I didn't wake you up, but I needed to call you with something time-sensitive. It couldn't wait."

"It's okay, I was up already just eating some breakfast. What is wrong?"

"Oh, nothing is *wrong* dear, just had some information for you that was important to transmit urgently. We are calling a pack meeting that will take place at noon. It is short notice obviously which is unfortunate, but it is mandatory due to the topic that will be discussed so I wanted to call you personally and inform you rather than sending a text."

"Noon today? Where do I need to go?" I ask her, trying to confirm the details.

"Just come to the house, we will be meeting there in the back, just like last time."

"Okay. I will be there. Thanks for calling, I'll see you in a little bit."

She gives her goodbyes and I end the call. Xan who has been silently monitoring me the whole call raises an eyebrow at me in question. So, I fill him in on what is going on. Once done eating I help clean up the remainder of the breakfast and even though I don't want to leave here I know that I need to go.

"Will you come back later? I was hoping to spend a little more time together and talk about a couple of things." Xan asks into my hair as he has me wrapped up tight in an embrace.

"Yes, I would like that. I will stop by my place after the meeting to grab a few things and then I will come back if that is alright."

He nods and after disentangling ourselves I head home to change out of these conjured pajamas and into something more suitable for the upcoming group event.

***

After I stopped by my place and cleaned myself up, I headed toward the MacGregor home for the meeting. I'm not sure what the meeting is about but anytime there is a mandatory meeting anyone who doesn't attend will suffer severe consequences. I've tried to avoid the pack as much as possible ever since Fallon was announced as the pack alpha. I already didn't want anything to do with him and now he is the man in charge of our entire pack, I can't stand the idea that he can give me orders that I would be required to obey. He has been going through and meeting with each of the pack members individually to connect with them and get a handle on issues facing us all. Luckily, he hasn't requested a meeting with me–yet–for all I care he can skip meeting with me. I would rather deal with any possible issues alone than be forced to meet with him one-on-one.

The crowd breaks out into whispered murmurs as Rowan–the late alpha's wife–walks toward the front of the crowd. People move out of her way allowing her room to pass. She comes to a stop at a small wooden platform and climbs onto it. Shortly after she gets situated the whispers stop as she assesses the crowd. Fallon approaches from who knows where and climbs the platform to join his mother.

"Thank you all for coming out tonight for this meeting, I know we sprung it on you all suddenly, but it is very vital to make this announcement," Rowan says.

There is quiet among the crowd now. Everyone watches with rapt attention as their formal alpha's mate addresses us all. Despite the passing of Angus, Rowan will still hold a position of honor and be revered by all.

Rowan grabs Fallon's hand and stares him in the eyes briefly before Fallon gives her a small reassuring nod that seems to settle whatever internal debate she is having.

Turning back toward us she says, "Finley, please come here."

I haven't heard any word about the content of tonight's meeting, it has been kept a closely guarded secret. So, the fact that she wants me to come to the stage makes me feel uncomfortable. What could she want me for? I will always respect and love Rowan, that doesn't change just because she raised some foul sons. I haven't been involved in a lot of the pack business the past few years, I've kept attending mandatory meetings and helping enough that I look unaffected, even though the entire group knows what happened with the MacGregor boys. Even though I am confused about why she wants me, I do as ask and move toward the front. People are back to talking quietly among themselves as I pass. I try to ignore their theories, not a reason to get in a tizzy about what this might be about, it's better to not make assumptions.

"Yes, Rowan?" I say to her when I reach the platform.

She sticks her hand out to me, and I take hold of it. "Please step up here, Finley dear."

I do as asked. I feel even more uncomfortable now, being elevated above everyone else and being put on display like this when no one told me anything about this ahead of time.

She positions me in between her and Fallon. I try to shuffle closer to her as if proximity to Fallon will infect me with the plague. I know it is probably immature, but I want to avoid him at all costs. I want nothing to do with the man who once was my best friend. Who once was my ride or die. My confidant in all secrets. My partner in crime anytime mischief was to be had. The man who gave the final blow to my cracked heart causing it to go from splintered to shattered. My attempts at getting some space are futile, there is nowhere to go to escape him no matter how desperate I am.

"As we all are aware, whenever a new alpha is elevated if they are unmated, they must take a mate within an allocated time following acceptance of their new role. This is something we have always required, and the purpose is to help establish a partner for the alpha who will help lead the pack as well as through continuing strong bloodlines."

My stomach drops, suddenly feeling like it's full of lead. This can't be happening. This can't be the reason they want me up here. They can't think I would go along with this. Sweat starts to coat my hands, face, and back. My breathing becomes difficult to keep consistent as panic starts to consume me.

"We asked you to gather so we could announce formally that I will be taking Finley Thomson as my mate at the next full moon celebration," Fallon exclaims to the crowd in an exuberant tone as if he didn't just drop a bomb and detonate my soul.

Thoughts race through my head. *Betrayal.* The word keeps circling back to me. He has betrayed me–again! It wasn't enough that my best friend completely obliterated my heart when I needed him the most but now, he is trying to force a connection I never would have wanted to have with him. After the cruelty he showed me and the abandonment I have to wonder if this is his way of punishing me. Is he trying to force me to love him? He couldn't have me when I chose his brother so now, he is trying to take the choice away from me to get what he wants. Anger starts to devour me as the word betrayal continues to toll in my head like a bell being struck repeatedly. I rip my hand away from Rowan who gives me a shocked look of confusion.

"NO!" I shout at the top of my lungs causing everyone to go silent.

"What do you mean no dear?" Rowan asked me like she couldn't possibly understand my refusal.

"No, exactly what I said. I will not become Fallon's mate. Not happening."

There are gasps from the crowd who start to buzz with outrage and questions amongst themselves.

"You do not get a choice in this Fin. I am the alpha. I am required to acquire a mate and you will be that mate." Fallon levels me with a glare that could destroy cities.

Shaking my head, I started to back away from Fallon who had moved closer to me when he was speaking. Before I can withdraw far enough to exit the platform he grabs me, wrapping an arm around my waist to cage me between the arm and his chest.

"No, I won't do it." I try to say it with conviction, but my voice involuntarily wobbles when I speak.

His body is pressed tightly to my body as he looks deeply into my eyes. I thought there was rage before but as his nostrils flare it seems to intensify tenfold. He moves his head closer to me and I worry he is going to try and force a kiss to my lips, but it turns out to be worse than that. He starts sniffing me furiously.

"Who?" He barks at me.

"Who what?" I ask.

"Who is he?" He continues sniffing me. "I can smell him on you, you're drowning in his scent."□

"It's none of your business Fallon!" I try to pull away from him, but he won't allow his hold to be broken.

"It is my business. You are *MINE*! You were always supposed to be mine! You are not getting out of this Finley. You know the laws of the pack. If you refuse me, you know you will be excommunicated by the pack. You will essentially be dead to us."

"Fine by me." I spit out as a retort.

My response only enraged him more. The fact that I would rather give up our pack, our family than be his mate than choose him. Pulling away from me, his body starts to vibrate. This is not good. The shift is trying to take over his body despite the fact you can visibly see he is trying to hold it back. He whistles loudly, gaining everyone's attention, and yells, "Time for a hunt!" Then he jumps from the stage shifting to his wolf form mid leap.

Chaos is the only way to describe the few minutes that follow his transformation. Several other men from our pack shift to their wolf forms as well and the group of them all take off running through the forest at full speed. Everyone else stares in the direction they took off in and breaks out in yells and a flurry of action.

Kai sprinted in my direction, coming to an abrupt stop next to me. With wide eyes, she exhaled a shaky breath and exclaimed, "What the hell just happened?"

I turned my face away from her to try to hide the hot tears that were starting to stream down my face. My eyes burn and the anger inside me builds infinitely stronger.

"He's going after Xan. He smelled him on me, and he was angry that I tried to reject him. He is going to hunt him down." Sniffling, I looked back at her. Her expression was horrified, eyes wide. "We can't let him get Xan; I have no doubt he would try to hurt him."

Resolve to harden, I pull my phone from my pocket. I dial Xan's number and wait while it rings. And rings. And rings. The panic I'm trying to hide is rising inside of me. *Pick up. Please pick it up.* The ringing ends and the voicemail message begins to play–*You've reached Alexander, leave me a message*–Beep. Frantically I leave him a message hoping he gets it before it's too late to protect him, "Xan, baby, if you are anywhere, we've been before together I need you to run! Go somewhere safe where you can hide for a bit until I can find you. There was an issue at the pack meeting, Fallon and several of the best trackers in the pack are trying to find you using the scent they caught off me. Please don't try to be a tough guy and face them. They're more than likely out for blood. I wouldn't be able to stand it if they hurt you, so please do as I ask. I will try to get them to calm down and I will contact you again in a while." I terminate the call and stuff the phone back into my pocket.

In anger, I stomp my way across the yard to where Rowan stands. She is staring in confusion in the direction her son just took off in. I'm completely livid right now and seeing as Fallon left, I'm going to take it out on the only person available to give my anger to. She knew this was going to happen.

"Seriously?!" I yell when I get in front of her. My hands fisted at my sides, shaking.

She turns to face me, and she doesn't seem to understand why I'm upset. She looks at me but doesn't say anything, waiting for me to continue my planned tirade.

"You knew he was going to do this today." I accuse her.

"Of course, I knew he was going to announce he wanted you as his mate. She confirmed what I already knew.

"You didn't think to stop him from doing this or at least warn me?"

Her head rears back slightly and shock crosses her face. "Why would I try to stop Fallon and you from becoming mated? I am happy to have you join our family, you've always been like a daughter to me Finley. You two used to be so close and it makes perfect sense. I always thought it should have been you two that got together rather than being with Callum. This is something to celebrate."

Is she delusional? Doesn't she know we had a falling out and don't talk or even make eye contact? Even if that was ignored, would she think it was okay for Fallon to try to make me his mate when I almost married his brother? That would make for uncomfortable family gatherings.

"He once was my best friend, but those days are over. He abandoned me when I needed him most and he showed his true feelings he had kept under wraps. He showed his loathing and belittled me when I found out about Callum cheating on me. His brother might have been the one who broke my heart, but Fallon broke my soul. It's too late to even reconcile the friendship we once had. I'm happily with someone else, and now Fallon is going to hunt him down!" Tears are welling in the corner of my eyes as I deliver this information. I tried to keep my voice level when I spoke but by the end, my voice had been cracking.

Kai rubs one hand down my back in soothing circles. "What are we going to do?" Kai asks me with determined grit.

"We aren't going to do anything. This is my problem. You're my best friend and I love you. But I'm the one who is going to end up being in trouble with the pack and most likely excommunicated if Fallon is to be believed. I won't have you being kicked out of the pack too. It's an integral part of being a shifter, being without a pack is like being without half a soul." There is no way I'd let her put her position in danger for me, no matter how scared I am.

"*I* am the only person in charge of *me*. I understand you want to protect me, but you are more important to me than any of these fuckers. Xan is yours which means I will protect him the same as I would protect you. They aren't going to get away with this. We need to track down Fallon and his cronies to put a stop to this before they get too far."

I don't want her to be involved and she knows that but also, I can't stop her. Once Kai is determined to do something there really is no use fighting her. Conceding to her, "Fine, but we need to shift. We aren't going after them like this. We will have better chances in our wolf forms."

Kai nods her head in agreement. With that, we both shift. It only takes a couple of minutes for us to transform. Kai to her white shaggy wolf and me to my ash brown one. The urges of the wolf are strong, fighting back the human nature we try hard to cling to in normal circumstances. I let the wolf guide me as her instincts take over, a calm destructive energy feels like it's now pulsing in my veins. We will tear apart anyone who tries to hurt Xan. *He is ours,* my inner wolf chants, *protect.*

I start running in the direction the guys took off earlier, with Kai closely trailing behind me. When we get to the end of the tree line, we both start sniffing, trying to gain the scent trail we need to follow. Once I feel confident that I have a lock on their trace, I run, faster than I ever had. Surprisingly Kai keeps up with me just as quickly.

Protect. It's like a song singing in my blood. *I will protect what is mine.*

Eleven

FALLON

When I learned I would be the new alpha of Fang I understood that would mean needing to take a mate, since it goes against bylaws to have an unmated alpha. Finley's face flashed across my mind as soon as I knew I was alpha. Becoming the leader gave me a chance to have something I've always wanted. She would be mine just as I always dreamed, she would be. This was the greatest opportunity of my life, even greater than being named alpha, she always meant more to me than pack politics. But this was the perfect opportunity to make all my dreams a reality.

When I discussed it with my mother, she was all for it. She knew how much Finley had always meant to me. She knew I was in love with Finley long before I even knew it and she knew the heartbreak and betrayal I felt when she started dating Callum. My mother loves Fin, and she never outright forgave Callum for what he did to hurt her because it meant she lost that future daughter-in-law.

Directly after the alpha challenge, I told my mom about my intentions to claim Finley as mine and she started helping me make plans and arrangements.

In the time since the breakup between Callum and Finley, she has only been on a few dates, and nothing had ever been serious. We weren't talking and she avoided me like I was a plague she would be contaminated by. Despite our lack of communication, I would regularly gather information about her and what she had been up to, especially about any dates she was going on.

I didn't personally follow her and keep tabs, but I tasked several pack members with helping with tracking her movements and interests. As the alpha's son, I was able to make the demand for their cooperation with little to no resistance. No one batted an eye or asked why I wanted them to help me follow her. They probably assumed it was something my father had asked me to manage in case she decided to seek retribution against Callum.

On more than one occasion when it seemed like things were going a little too well with a man, she started seeing I would intervene. Usually, that would look like having some guys from our pack doing some assignments such as finding dirt on the guy to blackmail him into breaking up with her. One of the times it was a little harder, we couldn't find any dark deeds to blackmail into getting our way, so a few of our shifters met him in a dark alley one night. The guy ended up getting every toe broken on one foot until he agreed to break it off. The agreement though was that he had to make it believable and not let her know that he was being coerced into dumping her. We kept an eye on him, and he stuck to his word, he dumped her, and even followed my orders to drive the knife deeper by telling her he met someone else and was in love. It is kind of a dick move to make her relive that moment of feeling inadequate, but my thought process was that maybe she would remember that she always had been enough for me. I thought that maybe it would drive her back to me, but I was wrong. After that she sequestered herself, no longer going on dates, only going out for work and to spend time with Kai.

Once she stopped going out on dates, I thought maybe the solitude would open her up to talking to me again. So, I may have put myself into various positions that caused us to have more frequent run-ins together so that the opportunity would be there. But again, this didn't work in my favor. It was like her hatred for me was too great. After all this time I still don't understand why she stopped spending time with me, it's not like I was the one who cheated on her and broke her heart. My brother is such a stupid idiot, he shouldn't have let himself be so blind to the treasure he had in Finley. She was perfect in every way, she was brilliant, beautiful, and had a super sexy body–one I intend to take full advantage of when she is my mate.

Everything was going according to the plan my mom and I laid out. We even planned the announcement ceremony and made sure that no one let Finley and her best friend Kai know what was happening. My mother called her and pretended the whole thing was an impromptu meeting so that way she would be there and not be skittish about attending. We knew it might be underhanded to spring this on her without discussing it with her or asking her myself, however with it being officially announced to the pack it is binding, she has to accept or leave the pack.

The plan was going great, she came to the meeting none the wiser, and I announced with my mother. But then when we were standing up on the platform and she started denying me, in my anger, my breathing turned ragged, and the deeper breathing caused me to pick up a scent. She had the smell of a man all over her. She reeked of his stench.

Anger flooded my entire body. She didn't just have his scent on her like someone she happened to spend time with, she smelled of his essence, it's someone she was intimately involved with. Whoever he is, touched what is *mine*, he touched *her*.

Before I could even realize what, I was doing, I rallied a group of our best trackers and hunters and we took off following the scent of the male, on a mission to find him. I might not know who he is yet, but we will find him soon and whoever he is, will no longer be of consequence. I haven't decided what we will do with him yet, it depends on his willingness to cooperate. I've gotten rid of countless others to make a path forward for myself, he won't stand in my way. I even got rid of my brother, for fuck's sake. He *was* cheating on her anyway, but when I overheard him on the phone with a girl talking about all the dirty things, he was going to do to her, I might have bribed Finley's professor to let class out early that evening. If she stayed in class for the normal allotment of time, she wouldn't have made it to the party to see what happened. So, I made sure to orchestrate the opportunity for her to catch my brother.

When she showed up at my house a crying mess after witnessing him cheating, I had planned to hold her and let her cry on my shoulder. I planned to show her my support and help her mourn their relationship. When she was ready to move on, I planned to swoop in and make her realize I had been there the whole time, ready and waiting for her. But when she showed up, I fucked it up, I couldn't help the venomous words that spewed from my mouth that night. I wanted her to hurt, the way I hurt. I wanted her to see how wrong a choice she had made, how stupid it was that she even started a relationship with Callum in the first place.

My stupid mouth had ruined a lot that night. My plans were derailed because instead of comforting her I hurt her. So, it had to happen this way. I had to spring this mating announcement on her to trap her. With time I knew she would accept it and grow to care for me again like she once did—hopefully even greater than she did before.

The first place the scent trail led us was to a nightclub. It's too early for the club to be open yet and the parking lot is empty. She must have been spending time with *him* here since we were able to find our way here, but it seems like a dead end. So, we went back to searching.

The trail we picked up from the club ended up leading to Finley's place. We had people go to each side of the place to make sure that this fucker couldn't try and run. Then I kicked in the front door and rushed inside. Her house still looks the same as it always has.

Shortly after Finley started college, she started renting this house she had found in a newspaper ad. Eventually, the older woman who owned it decided to sell the house and because Finley was living in it and still had a valid lease, they worked out a deal for Finley to purchase it.

The house is only a smaller two-bedroom, one-bath home. It is a bit of an older place, but the upkeep has been maintained thoroughly. The only reason the woman sold it was because she didn't want the stress of taking care of the house anymore. Finley bought it and when she and Callum got engaged, she started making big plans for this to be their home together.

Even though I was angry at the time about them being together I still came over a lot to help them when they did projects on the house. We redid the paint in most of the house, stripped and redid the stain on the hardwood floors, and a lot of little things throughout the place. I helped create this home that she wanted to share with my brother but when I worked on this house, I imagined it as *our* house. I pictured coming home to her at the end of every day, eating meals in the dining area that we cooked together, watching movies curled up in the living room, and having hot passion-filled sex in every room.

Her denying me–this time publicly–makes me want to burn this place to the ground. No other man should be able to reap the rewards of the work I did to make this a home. No other man should be able to make a life with her here, to fuck her here.

Thinking about it just makes me feel even more worked up and ready to destroy anything and everything.

Markus and Quinn walk through the door and now that I'm no longer the only one inside we start walking through the house as a unit. Checking each of the rooms for the mystery man.

The house was empty, but I got a stronger whiff of his scent in her bedroom. Fury pulses inside me at this. I walk back into her room and start looking for any evidence of him. Nothing seems out of place; it doesn't seem like there are any of his belongings here.

The bed is made, and I know Finley isn't a morning person, so this leads me to believe she didn't sleep here last night. She must have stayed at *his* place. I'm not sure which idea is worse, him being in this house, or her staying the night with him.

Several minutes of rummaging through all her crap and I haven't found a lot. There are a few items of clothing on the floor by her closet. It isn't like Finley to leave a mess lying around, it isn't her normal habit. If she stayed the night with him, maybe she had to change clothes before coming to our pack meeting, and if she was in a hurry that could explain the mess. Bending down to retrieve the clothes, I bring them to my nose and smell them. The scent on them is stronger than it was on her at the meeting. These were recently worn around him.

I toss the clothes to Markus who smells them, then tosses them to Quinn. They are our strongest trackers and now that we have a stronger source, we should be able to get a better trail to follow.

We emerge from the house and rally all the guys who were outside guarding the exterior of the house in case of a potential escape attempt.

"He's not here," I announce.

"We got a better scent source to track and are going to get back to following it," Quinn says.

Markus moves closer to me, "Orders?"

I look over my shoulder in the direction of the house, then move my eyes back to him, "Burn it." With that demand, they jump into action and do just that.

Twelve

Xan

This morning ever since Finley left for her meeting, I've been missing her so bad it hurts. I feel pathetic. How did I go from a badass warlock, someone that you wouldn't want to cross paths within a dark alley, to this lovesick puddle of mush? It bothers me to feel so completely desperate for her presence, but also, I'm so willingly gone for her. She is *everything*.

Either way, I am counting down the hours, minutes, and seconds until I can see her again. I'm in my office trying to work. This is supposed to be serious work. I have a list so long of orders that I'm backed up. Today I am making 'minor' curses and hexes, nothing too intense, and all temporary. They are all things I have experience making so the process isn't foreign to me, but because the ingredients can be dangerous if not properly handled, I need to give my full attention.

So far, I've made it through three of the ten on my to-do list. Interestingly enough those three hexes were all for the same buyer, I have a sneaking suspicion that they are pretty upset about something. Thinking of what schemes they might be plotting makes me chuckle a little. Every once in a while, I do a more serious curse or hex, but for the most part, I just like to help create the ones that are meant for minor mischief rather than for creating fatalities or that have life-altering repercussions.

Ever since I was a young boy, I always enjoyed mischief and chaos. I often found ways to get into other people's business because my life was so boring. When I was only twelve, a few local friends and I ran a small operation where we would get paid to spy on people or implement pranks. It was more for fun than for money, but it ended up being pretty lucrative for our age.

After I put away the finished potions I just created, I grab the ingredients for my next project, when there is a loud *BANG* from somewhere in the building. Setting down the items I was holding, I walked over grabbed a couple of protective items, and stuffed them in my pocket, unlike mortals I do not own weapons for protection, I rely on magic.

As I walk toward the office door, it bursts open before I can get there. In runs several disheveled-looking men, all of them sizing me up with their eyes. The one in the front is a redhead and he looks furious. I don't recognize any of them, my first thought is that perhaps they are people who were cursed by a customer and are unhappy about it. If that's the case they are going to be sorely disappointed, I don't give a shit who my customers use their curses or hexes on, I just care about getting paid.

One of the men towards the back steps forward, sniffing so hard and fast that it is causing him to make huffing noises. "It's him, alpha."

Alpha, that word brings me pause. These men are shifters of some sort because shifters are the only ones who use alpha as a title for their leader. Witches and vampires use the title of coven master as the name for their leader. Many other types of supernaturals don't have organized groups like those few, an example of that is how the squatch species prefer to live solitary lives among nature.

The red-headed man stalks closer toward me, "It's him alright. His smell was all over Finley." He all but growls out the words.

"Finley? What do you gentlemen have to do with Finley?" I ask, eyebrows furrowed.

"Finley is going to be the alpha's mate!" A man at the rear yells.

The statement turns my mood to ire. She is *mine*. She is not going to be anything to this asshole. Finley and I are happy. There is no way she would agree to this. On top of that, whether she knows it or not, I'm her fate's blessed mate. That isn't something taken lightly. I haven't told her yet what I discovered but I intended to talk to her about it tonight when she wasn't stressed about the pack meeting, she had to go to.

"The fuck she is! Fuck off. She is my mate. She wouldn't be anything to the 'alpha'." I try to imbue the term alpha with as much distaste and sarcasm as I can, to show how I feel about him thinking he deserves someone so special as Finley–not that I'm deserving of her either but that's not truly the point.

The redhead lets out an angered growl, "Snatch him, Benny."

With the order issued, the man who I am assuming is Benny bolts toward me lightning-quick and tries to grab my arms. I try to fight him off, I'm not going to let them do anything to me. As I work to free my arms, another man joins Benny in restraining my arms. Between the two of them working together, my fight is futile. Before long they had my arms wrenched behind my back, and someone produced zip ties from somewhere and secured my arms.

"Which MacGregor son are you anyways? The youngest, the one who broke her heart, or the one who was bitter about not getting a taste?" I already know that the brother named Fallon won the alpha challenge, but I ask anyway to remind him he hasn't gotten what I have.

He walks closer, only stopping when he is in my face, with a hard hit to my gut, he replies, "Fallon. The one who is going to steal your so-called *mate*." He sneers in distaste looking around my office. "Let's burn this place boys. If he is alive by the time, we are done with him, we don't want him to be back in the world creating evil as warlocks generally do."

He walks over to the table where I was just working and with one arm, clears the table by flinging his arm at all the objects. Items fly in all directions, crashing to the ground. Bottles and vials busting, glass going everywhere. One of his henchmen starts pulling down grimoires and tossing them into a pile in the center of the room, sometimes taking the time to wrench pages from the books to rip them apart, and other times just throwing them down. Those took me years to compile, all that knowledge going to waste, it is despicable!

There is nothing I can do as I am held by the two men who guard me, as I watch them destroy my life's work. They load me into the back of an SUV and as we pull away, I see my club burning in the distance.

****

Not long after we left my home and business burning in the rearview, they shoved a pillowcase over the top of my head, some real freaking geniuses they are. It feels like we have been driving for fucking ever. Since all I can see is the faint trickle of light that is coming through the tiny, knitted holes in the fabric, I can't tell if we are driving somewhere that is far away, or if they are trying to toy with me by driving for so long.

Despite them thinking they are tough and brutal, I don't fear them, and since the driving is taking so long, I decided I might as well take a little nap. It feels like as soon as I start to fall asleep, they wake me up. I'm assuming we must be pulling into a driveway somewhere because the car is hitting lots of small bumps and I can hear the crunch of gravel under the tires before we creep to a halt.

"Markus, help Benny drag his ass to the house," Fallon commands his lackeys.

The door closest to me is wrenched open, the hinges squealing with the jarring motion. The pillowcase they used as a hood to blind me is torn away. The light is painful after being in the semi-darkness and I force my eyes closed momentarily to block it out. Hands come up and grab my upper arms, pulling me roughly from the car. Opening my eyes again, I try to take in all my surroundings and make some type of sense of where I am.

We are standing in the driveway of a two-story house with a wrap-around porch, and woods surrounding the property. Not the lair of a villain or a hideout for criminals. It looks like a family home. I can almost picture parents chasing unruly kids across the lawn on a sunny weekend day, giggles tearing out of the children as they dodge their parents.

The men walk through the front door into the house, and I obediently follow. Once we are in the foyer I gaze around and am met with exactly what I believed. This is a family home. Photos are lining the walls down the hall. Photos that I am assuming are of the MacGregor family, I'm guessing this because there is a younger version of Fallon depicted in the images. As we continue to walk I even spot photos of Finley. Some containing her are with Fallon when they are small. Others are the entire MacGregor family and include her. At the end of the hall is even a photo of Finley with her hand extending toward the camera, showing off an engagement ring, while a man–Callum–has himself wrapped around her body, cheek to cheek smiling brightly. What a piece of shit he is, here he is in this photo looking like the luckiest man on the planet, happy as anyone can ever hope to be, and yet he cheated on Finley and broke her heart. Did he ever actually care or was he good at performing?

A red-headed woman walks around the corner into the room we stopped in. She eyes me up and down before approaching us. "So, you found him?" She asked, the question directed at Fallon.

With a deep scowl on his face, Fallon nods his head in affirmation.

"Where is Fin?" He asks the woman while looking around like she is going to appear any moment.

"She left." The woman looks nervous when she admits this information.

"What do you mean she left?!" He yells.

"After you and the guys left to go after him," she gestures to me by flinging an accusing arm in my direction, "Finley confronted me and when she was done, she and Kai shifted and fled. We tried to stop her from leaving, but most of the pack had already left at that point and you took most of your men with you that could have helped in the situation. It was mostly just a few of us older members and women left here, we weren't able to detain her."

It shouldn't be possible, but Fallon starts to appear even more irate than he previously was. Pacing back and forth across the room. Not saying a word. No one makes eye contact with him during this as if they don't want to incur his wrath. Suddenly he charges at the wall and punches hard, leaving a hole behind in his fit of rage.

The noise must have drawn the attention of others within the house. Momentarily two figures emerge into the room. I instantly recognize them, Fallon's brothers, Callum and Knox. Both look first to Fallon, then to the hole in the wall, finally letting their eyes settle on me. Knox, who is looking at me inquisitively as I'm standing here restrained, turns toward his mother, "Mum, what is going on?" Then he nods his head in my direction and asks, "Who's he?"

She opens her mouth to respond, then closes it, her eyes move slowly back to Fallon as if she is trying to decide the best way to explain this situation without making her middle son angrier than he already is. Before she can decide what to say I cut her off, "My name is Alexander Moretti, I'm Finley's *mate*." I let a toothy smirk grace my face as I shoot daggers in Callum's direction. I want the look to express all the thoughts I don't bother giving voice to at the moment–that Finley is *mine*, that I know who he is, and that he will never again get a chance with her.

"*STOP* saying that!" Fallon growls as he stalks closer to me, putting us face to face. "She will be my mate. You are nothing to her. She might have wasted some time with you and spread her legs for you like a fucking whore, but in time you will be nothing. She will forget you and nothing will be more satisfying to me, than thinking about how wrong you were, when I drive my cock deep inside her, branding her from the inside out." He sneers after he finishes his diatribe.

"So, you plan to think about me when you're balls deep in her? What a strange thing to say, but I guess if you are that attracted to me, I am flattered." I taunt, letting my lip curl up on one side.

That little jibe I made earned me another gut punch, but it was so worth it. If I am going to be held captive and have to listen to him spout bullshit I might as well be able to have a little fun with him in the meantime. Rather than showing pain, I chuckle, and raise back up to my full height, to maintain eye contact with him.

"You son of a b–" He is interrupted before he can finish with the useless name-calling, but I know that I got under his skin. Goal achieved, I mentally high-five myself.

"What the hell Fallon?" Knox demands as he positions himself in between Fallon and me.

"I'm with Knox, explain yourself, now!" Callum cuts in.

The flames of Fallon's rage seem to bank higher at being told to explain himself to his brothers. I imagine Callum sees no issue with the demand, being the big brother, he is probably used to being in charge but Fallon being the alpha means he is of higher ranking. Before any further argument can ensue, their mother starts talking.

"You boys were at the meeting and witnessed what happened when Fallon announced claiming Finley for his future mate. She was persistent about not wanting to commit to that. When she was standing by your brother he scented a male scent on her, he said it was really strong. He was a little emotional and all about what happened. So, he and a few of the other guys tracked the scent to this fella and decided to bring him here. But I don't know much else..." She trails off at the end and kind of surveys the room, not sure where to focus her attention, trying to decide how deep of crap everyone is in now.

"What are you to Finley?" Callum asks me as he tilts his head slightly to the side.

"As I said before, Finley is my mate, my *fates blessed mate.*" I raise one eyebrow in a challenge at him, daring him to try and beat me.

"That's not—that's not possible." He replies but his voice lowers when he speaks the words, like he lacks conviction despite uttering the words.

"Fates blessed mates are very rare and highly unlikely." Their mom interjects.

"Rare, yes. Highly unlikely, also yes. But it's still true. The moment I saw Finley I felt drawn to her. She was the brightest star in the night sky. A beacon of light in a storm. I could think of nothing else. She consumed me whole before she even spoke a word to me. She brought out feelings I'd never experienced. My desire for her and compulsion to be near her, has only continued to exponentially increase. It left me perplexed and trying to grapple with what was happening. Last night I used blood magic to try to gain insight into the situation and it indicated we are fate's blessed mates. It wasn't something I could have theorized because I know how rare it is, but I wouldn't change it for anything."

Fallon releases a joyless laugh. "Sure. Of course, we would trust what a warlock has to say. It's not like they don't enjoy chaos and being sinister." Sarcasm drips off every word he says.

"It doesn't matter what you think about me or the stereotypes you assign to warlocks. Your opinions won't change the truth of the situation, nor will it make Fallon love you." I retorted, growing more irritated every second I had to spend with this unrelenting and delusional man.

Knox, who has been quietly observing the confrontation finally makes his presence known again, "What are you going to do with him? If Finley and Kai go looking for him, eventually they will return here."

"I am still making my plans. But for now, I need to move him somewhere else for safekeeping, just for the time being. Callum, give me the keys to your cabin."

"You're going to take him to my cabin? Why do you want to bring him there?"

"No, Markus and Benny are going to take him to your cabin. You're going too and will keep an eye on him for me. Do not lose him. If he gives you any difficulty or too much lip, feel free to rough him up a little, as long as he remains recognizable for a little while longer." Then he swivels toward Knox, "You are going to join me for some strategizing. I imagine it won't be long until Finley finds out he is missing or sees what I've done to that nightclub he owns and her house. She will be coming, and I don't plan on letting her get away this time."

"What did you do to her house?" Callum asked him with concern shining bright in his eyes.

"I think the better question is what house?" Fallon releases a dark laugh and shares a knowing look with his men.

With those ominous orders handed out, we split up. Benny and Markus start shoving me back out the front door, stuffing me back into the SUV once again. Thankfully this time sans pillowcase for a blindfold.

Benny and Markus took the front seats, leaving Callum to sit in the rear with me. He shakes his head and huffs in irritation as we pull out of the driveway. "This is idiotic." He mumbles, barely audible to me, but if I could hear it, then the shifters in the front definitely could hear it since shifters have excellent hearing.

Thirteen

FINLEY

After Kai and I left the MacGregor house we tried to catch up with the guys, but we were too far behind. We ended up doubling back and getting Kai's SUV so we could drive instead of being in our wolf forms, running back to town would have been doable but it would have been unpleasantly tiring. I've tried several more times to reach Xan on the phone and haven't gotten through to him. I've caved and even tried calling Fallon a few times too, to see if I can talk him down from whatever fresh hell, he thinks he is going to attempt to unleash, every time I call it goes to voicemail after one ring, and he is rejecting the calls.

"Where to first?"

"Remember the nightclub we went to?" When she nods her head I continue, "Go there. Xan owns that club, and he has a loft apartment upstairs."

She hits the gas, and we speed off toward town, definitely exceeding the speed limit.

When we get to where the club should be we are met with the sight of the building partly burnt down. The fire department is on-site working to battle the blaze of flames. I fling the passenger door open and drop down from the vehicle. Sprinting as fast as I can, I make my way over to the fire chief.

"What happened?" I ask him, gesturing toward the building.

"We got called in for a building fire about ten minutes ago, we were called right after the fire started, however with the extent of the damage, it appears an accelerant was used. Look, ladies, you need to leave the premises. There is too much going on right now, the fire is difficult to extinguish, and it is a dangerous environment at present." He tries to dismiss us and swivels back toward the building.

I race forward after the fire chief and grab his arm. He whorls toward me with a questioning expression, most likely confused about why I am still hounding him when he has work to do.

"Please. This is my boyfriend's place. He has a loft above the club where he lives. Is he okay?"

The chief shakes his head slowly and my gut drops like a rock being thrown from a cliff. No, this can't be happening, he can't be–

Before I can finish the spiraling panic of thoughts the chief interrupts me, "We have cleared the building, and we found no survivors or victims. It was empty."

I think that is the best news I've ever been given in my life. The worry of him being gone, permanently, was going to tear me apart. We haven't been together long but my feelings for Xan are so strong, stronger than I felt even about Callum in our entire relationship. If he was dead, I would die too, maybe not physically but I would die emotionally and mentally. If he was gone and I had to live without him it would destroy me, I could feel it in my soul. I don't know how I could even explain it to someone if I needed to, but I felt inexplicably bound to him.

I flung my arms out and tightly wrapped them around the chief. This might have felt weird if he was some random person, I didn't know but I've known the chief since I was a little girl. He may be a human, but he is dedicated to fairness and equality for all. He has long been established as a friend to the pack, and on several occasions helped with problems that arose between the pack and community officials when they behaved in a discriminative fashion.

The hug was unplanned and honestly surprised me as well as the chief. After a brief couple of seconds, I release the chief and he seems like he is about to ask me something when his radio goes off.

"Chief!" Crackles over the radio.

"You got me."

"We got another fire across town. Is your team available to head there or do I need to dispatch another truck?"

His brows knit together before he responds to the operator. "We are wrapping up here. Send another unit to get started and I will meet them there. Where is the location?"

One hand on his hip, the other on the radio, he stands there and listens as the operator gives the address of my home. It's completely shocking and even more confusing. What is happening and why? How is there a fire at my house? I'm not even there to tempt fate with my terrible cooking skills that often cause burnt dinners and a house full of smoke.

He gives an affirmation to the operator letting them know he will be headed to the scene, then he turns and makes eye contact with me. There is a question in his gaze.

"I do not know about what is happening there. The last time I was at home was earlier this morning for a few minutes and everything was fine."

He gives a sharp nod and then starts running to his SUV, after a few steps he turns his head to look behind me, "You want to ride with me?"

I glance back at Kai, and she nods vigorously before saying, "Go. I will meet you there."

With her approval, I jog to the SUV and climb in.

***

We pull up to my home and the scene is complete chaos. If it is possible, it looks worse than the nightclub did. The sight that meets us is the entire destruction of the place I am most comfortable and safe. A house that holds many memories, good and bad, is now a house no longer.

The unit that was dispatched has just arrived and firefighters are running back and forth between their truck and my house, setting up their equipment. There are shouts and everyone seems to know the role to play, except me. All I can do is stare at the burning remains and watch as they try to contain the destruction.

After a while the fire is out and everyone is packing up. Kai and I are still at the edge of the yard standing in the street watching. She and I both have been trying to go over possibilities while waiting for answers.

The truck jumps to life and the crew starts to drive away. As the truck pulls out, the chief walks toward us, a deep frown marring his face.

"So, we have the fire put out. There will continue to be some smoldering for a while. They did a full sweep of the premises and there was no one in the house, as we all previously believed. There was something concerning however, the fire was intentional. There was evidence of an accelerant being used to start and grow the fire. There was also one location that is the source of the fire; it appears that the fire originated in the master bedroom."

He pulls out his work cell phone and shows me some photos. He flips to a photo that once was my bedroom. Pointing out the location the fire originated he asks me, "What was previously here before the fire?"

My eyes meet Kai's briefly before I answer the chief, "That is where my bed sat."

The next half hour was spent answering questions to the chief about my house, about any suspicions I have about who would have started the fire and why–of course I told him that Fallon has lost his mind and he is probably behind it.

As the chief's truck starts to disappear in the distance I turn back to Kai, I'm sure she can tell just from my look all the things I'm feeling. Anger has taken a large toll on my emotional energy lately, but fear is threatening to break me at this moment. I'm so worried about Xan. Is he alive? Is he injured and if so to what extent? Where is he? What does Fallon intend to do to him? Fear aside other questions are floating through my mind as well. Does Fallon think I would ever agree to be his mate with him pulling a stunt like this? Has he become so mentally unstable that he thought this would work out in his favor? I thought his obsession with me ended a long time ago, around the time he kicked me out when I needed him when he told me how stupid I was for being with his brother, he seemed like he hated me at the time. But I guess I was wrong. Has he been silently building up to this the entire time? Was what pushed him over the edge seeing me happy with Xan or was it something else? All questions will probably go unanswered.

***

We spent a while at Kai's place trying to come up with reasonable next steps. The longer that Xan has been missing, the harder I'm finding it to be reasonable. My body feels so full of rage that I feel like it's vibrating inside of me, shaking my core foundation. I'm starting to realize that I would do anything to recover him safely, to protect him, to get retribution.

Kai and I already agreed that we were done with the pack after what happened at the meeting and how no one intervened in the shit show that was taking place. No one stood up for me or tried to rein in Fallon's crazy. Their lack of intervention makes them complicit and whether they intended it or not, they are now my enemy. I will no longer treat them as the friends they were, and they will not be spared any of my wrath or fury.

Our agreement on the future treatment of our former pack is what led us to our current situation. We are standing on the outskirts of the perimeter surrounding the MacGregor family home. We plan to stakeout the property for a while to see if they return here with Xan, and if not, we will wait until we see one of Fallon's accomplices at which point, we will make our move, snatch the perpetrator, and take him to a different location to *ask some questions*–maybe some light torture if necessary.

We've been hiding in the tree line for a couple hours so far and the passing of time is making me more frustrated. There has been no sign of Xan, so he hasn't been transported back here and there has also been no return of Fallon.

"Stop pacing, you're going to attract attention," Kai said with a sideways glance in my direction.

Her demand made no difference to me. The pacing wasn't remedying anything, I knew that, but I felt like there was too much energy buzzing inside myself and if I didn't do something to expend it from my body, I was going to lose my mind.

Sitting here observing the property and waiting for something was starting to get to me when finally, I saw a familiar car pull up. Only one person was driving the car, and it wasn't Fallon.

I quietly signaled to Kai. I was able to garner her attention quickly since she was on high alert. This mission we were on proved to me that stakeouts were not a favorite activity for me, but Kai excelled at it. She seemed to thrive and was in complete control of her emotions, unlike me.

The car came to a stop in the driveway close to the house. We crept closer as silently as we could manage in our human forms. The car turned off and Benny stepped out before locking the door. Benny happens to be one of the pack members closest to Fallon, always trying his best to impress and gain praise. This is just what we need. Turning to face Kai, I gave her the look to signify this was it, time to try our hand at wolfnapping.

With the silent communication completed between us, we both leaped forward, our bodies transforming mid-air into our wolf forms. Benny, who had been distracted by something on the driver's side of the car, didn't notice us until it was too late, we had a significant advantage in time.

Kai charged forward coming straight at him while I held back only momentarily, this was an intentional tactic to make him think she was the predator to worry most about. He changed into his wolf form but by the time his transformation was complete Kai was upon him, teeth bared by both as they started to fight. With him distracted by her, I approached with determined confidence, when I reached him, he barely had time to turn his head before I grabbed his throat between my jaws, and with the hold around his neck, I forced him to the ground in a position of submission. I held him there for several minutes, face to the ground, silently letting him know who the dominant force was, letting him know not to fuck around.

When we were in the pack, we could always communicate telepathically with our other pack members whenever we were all in wolf form. Having left the pack I wasn't sure if I would be able to use that link to speak to Kai or not, and if I did would Benny still be able to understand our conversation? It was something we would have to test out to know for sure.

I want vanilla ice cream with lots of sprinkles in a dog bowl, I thought toward Kai.

Her chuffing noise was her response. Benny, who I no longer had my jaws around but still had pinned to the ground was looking at us with a blank expression. I purposefully said something weird so I could watch for a possible reaction from him. I figured that if he heard he would act confused or curious but judging by his neutral look, he hadn't caught wind of what was being said mentally. We were no longer connected to the Fang pack but were connected to our new pack.

Change back. At my orders, Kai transformed back to human form, and I followed suit. Then I instructed Benny to do the same.

Once we were all back into human form, I hoisted Benny to a standing position. He was considerably bigger than me, big for a male of the pack anyway, which is how Benny had become an enforcer. It was a little shocking I was able to single-handedly pick him up and control him, the adrenaline I was experiencing probably had something to do with it.

"We have questions, and you are going with us to answer them," I said to Benny with a tone that promised the potential for malice if he didn't cooperate.

***

We pulled up to the desolate rundown building on the outskirts of town and Kai put the vehicle in park. I unfastened my seatbelt with rapt speed and as I jumped out, I hollered, "I'll check it out, stay here with Benny until I come back."

Following the cracked sidewalk from the street, I ran up the front steps. I halted outside the door momentarily while I took a deep whiff of the air, trying to determine if I smelled anyone here recently. There didn't appear to be any recent visitors to the building, I could usually smell lingering scents for at least a week or so, meaning the building was most likely empty–but I would take a look inside to be sure.

Slowly pushing the unlocked front door open, I walked inside. The interior of the building has never been renovated in the duration of time the pack has owned it. The outside of the house makes the place look abandoned–shutters hanging from the windows from where they have become unhinged in certain areas, cracked glass on several of the street-facing windows, cracks in the sidewalk leading to the front door, an overgrown garden that no one has tended in years. It would be hard to believe the inside could be worse, but it is true. All the floors have been stripped down to the concrete, which is stained in many places with blood—some were there before the pack purchased the building and some were added after. No lights could be found inside causing it to be perpetually dark inside. The roof was also damaged and leaking, creating a mildew smell throughout the entirety of the space. The only furniture within these walls were items designed to be utilized for torture—long sturdy tables with bindings attached to all four corners to allow someone to be strapped down, chairs with arm cuffs attached, and shelves of tools to pry information from the prey.

Pack business was mostly on the up and up, however, every once in a while, there would be some unsavory things that needed to happen. Usually, this only would happen if someone did something to harm a shifter or the pack. Our leaders have never taken kindly to those who would go out of their way to cause harm or have ill intent, it was their duty to protect us.

After a thorough sweep of the small decrepit building, I confirmed my theory that it was empty. Walking back outside to the SUV, where Kai dutifully waited for me as I requested, I went straight to the trunk where we had stowed away Benny. I opened the trunk and grabbed Benny, who had his arms bound behind his back, and hauled him out of the vehicle. After his feet were on the sidewalk, I gave him a firm shove between his shoulder blades, and gave the forceful command, "Walk and don't stop until I tell you."

We led him up the sidewalk and had him stop in front of a couple of stairs on the porch so that we could assist him up since he was blindfolded.

"Where did you bring me?" He asked with a slight tremor of fear in his voice.

"You'll see soon enough, until then, be quiet."

Kai opened the front door and entered first with Benny and I following quickly behind her. She glanced at Benny and then she nodded her head toward the chair with the arm bindings, giving me a silent question. I nodded my head in agreement, and we tossed Benny into the chair where she promptly unbound his hands from behind his back and refastened them to the chair arms. Once he was secure Kai took a knife from her belt and sliced off his blindfold.

The revelation of where we were caused visible fear to shudder through Benny. He took in his surroundings and paled. His eyes started to have a slight glistening to them as if he was going to start crying and begging for his life. Something about that substantially improved my mood. The person and creature I am, wouldn't normally revel in instilling fear in others but I felt the shift in myself as soon as the pack let Fallon get away with the bullshit from the last meeting. They no longer matter to me; I want to make them prone at my feet to grovel for forgiveness and their lives. Somewhere in the back of my mind, I knew it was wrong to find joy in these feelings, but I couldn't find the capacity to care at the moment. They created this monster in me, and I had no qualms about unleashing it and showing them what they made me into.

Indignation was burning hot, coursing through my body. With little to no thought, I had partially shifted my hand, claws extended from my fingertips but otherwise left my hand in human form. I'd never been able to do a partial shift before, even when I tried with all the power in me. The fact that I was able to so easily complete it now, with no thought, was either a sign of my power growing, or maybe it was an indication of how volatile I was feeling. With most shifters, they can be in human form or their alternate form, the vast majority of us cannot shift partially at will, only the most powerful among us, usually this is only witnessed in alphas.

Not willing to look a gift horse in the mouth at this time, I decided to worry about this new development at a later time.

Slowly I approached Benny, each step I took towards him felt like it was a taunt. For the entirety of my life, I was of what I would consider average confidence, I had my moments of doubt like everyone, but I also never felt overly confident to the point of it being false bravado. But seeing Benny shake more with each movement, I felt like I was a god, and he was merely a barnacle in the depths of the ocean.

When I was standing directly in front of him, I brought my face inches away from his. Taking my pointer finger on my clawed hand, I gently caressed his bare forearm. It wasn't the caress of a lover; it was a silent promise of what was to come.

"Where does Fallon have Xan?"

Benny cast his eyes to the side before answering and claiming he didn't know. We both knew that was complete bullshit and he had to know we wouldn't fall for it. But that's the game he wanted to play, so we would play the game he set into motion.

I dug the tip of a claw into his arm, breaking the skin, and impaling about half an inch into his flesh.

With my voice lethally quiet, I said, "That was the wrong answer, Benny."

As I started to drag that claw further up his arm, he started to wail with pain. My movements were methodical as I continued to drag my finger up his arm as slowly as physically possible, making the pain continue at a tortuous rate.

"Try again," I demanded of him.

He was whimpering, as blood was dripping down his forearm and pooling on the floor. You could see the battle taking place in his mind, he was trying to debate whether to give up his disturbed leader or to continue with my interrogation techniques. The moment his choice was decided he let loose a breath and said, "Callum owns a cabin in the Marion Woods. Fallon took him there."

We went back and forth for several more minutes, me trying to determine where in the Marion Woods this cabin was located and how to get there, and Benny adamantly denying knowing how to get there. His repeated denial of knowing details was all the confirmation I needed to verify he had outlived his usefulness.

"Thank you for all the help you've given to me, Benny." I smiled at him, but it was an unkind, cruel smile of a predator.

He was vigorously nodding his head and asking about being uncuffed from the chair when I reached forward. Placing one hand on each of his cheeks I gripped his face. While maintaining eye contact I swiftly and forcefully snapped his neck. He instantly stilled and slumped to the side, causing the chair to tip over and clatter to the floor.

"What are we going to do with his body?" Kai asked me as we approached the front door to exit the building.

"Leave it. If anyone from Fang comes here, I want them to find it. I want them to know what awaits them."

With that, we strolled out of the shithole house and drove away to regroup. It was time to bring in reinforcements that I knew I could trust; the ones Xan would trust.

Fourteen

Finley

I t had been a couple of hours since we finished our interrogation of Benny. When we left the building, I immediately placed a call to Hadeon. He was one of Xan's closest friends, but he was also a very intimidating and intensely scary vampire. I told him everything that had happened, all the locations that Kai and I searched, and the information we gained from Benny, and after only a couple minutes we had plans to meet at the edge of Marion Woods which was closest to our town of Silver Ridge.

The GPS let us know we were approaching the coordinates we had programmed into it. Hadeon had insisted on using latitude and longitude coordinates for our meet point, so there was no confusion on where exactly we would all amass.

Up ahead there were a couple of cars already parked and Kai pulled up behind the car belonging to Leora, a cute little hatchback that was lime green with daisy stickers on it–the vehicle seemed fitting for the whimsical fairy.

We exited the SUV and approached the group. Ry and Leora were huddled together, whispering to each other, as Ry gently rubbed up and down Leora's arms as if trying to soothe her. Hadeon was standing stock still as if his body was empty, while his mind was planning and calculating every possible outcome. I knew some of Hadeon's history, but being a vampire who has been alive for a long time, I knew there would be plenty I didn't and probably wouldn't know about him. However, I did know he had been in many battles throughout his long life and had led quite a few of those himself. Then there was Alder. I've never seen him look so strange. His long legs were encased in military-style cargo pants with pockets stuffed to the brim with items. He had hiking boots on, which was probably a good idea since we didn't know where exactly this cabin was or how long we would be searching the woods. He had on a long-sleeved shirt despite the warm temperature. None of that was the strange part. The weird part was the fact that he was wearing a safari-style hat, with a mesh netting hanging over his face, covering from his head to the upper part of his torso. He also had tons of white sunblock clumped onto his face, not rubbed in well enough to hide. As we approached the group, I saw Alder take out a can of bug spray and start spraying it all over himself with an intensity that his clothing was starting to be visibly wet from the act.

When we were a few feet in front of the group, I saw Hadeon turn stalk still and take several inhalations before suddenly appearing in front of Kai and me. The handful of times I've spent time with Hadeon while with Xan hadn't been enough time for me to get used to the vampire's speed. Most of the time he moved the same as a human, only moving with his vampire speed when he deemed it appropriate. So, I was momentarily taken off guard by his unseen approach.

Kai stumbled back a couple of steps before catching her balance, and yelling, "What the hell!?"

Hadeon started circling me while inhaling deeply.

"I smell blood on you," he calmly stated before asking, "Are you injured?"□

Shooting a quirky grin in Kai's direction, showcasing the amusement I felt in reaction to her fear of Hadeon, then responded with, "It's not mine." Before explaining how we got the info about this potential location of Xan's sequestering and that the blood was the informant.

Once Hadeon was satisfied with the explanation he nodded his head in the direction of his companions, and we all headed in their direction.

Kai had never met them before today, but I had told her about all of them. She was introduced to them all, but I noticed her eyes kept lingering on Alder. But she wasn't looking at him with curiosity or politeness, there was a sneer intact on her face. He appeared a little strange right now, but I didn't feel like it was too out of character for him to be a little eccentric.

"Al, what's with the getup?" I asked him.

A sheepish look came over his face before Ry gave him a friendly pat on the shoulder and responded in his stead. "Don't you know? Our resident squatch is allergic to nature!" Then he breaks out in a fit of laughter.

"What are you talking about?"

Alder huffed in annoyance before further explaining, "I'm very sensitive to sunlight, it can cause hives very easily for me. I'm also allergic to poison ivy, oak leaves, bees, mosquitoes, hay, fleas, several species of birds, and ferns, honestly, the list is much longer than that, but I want to leave time for the inevitable ridicule."

I tried to contain the humor of the situation, but I failed, and a small chuckle still escaped me. "No wonder you live in town rather than in the wilderness like most of your kin."

"Well, that and the fact that I don't like solitude." He frowned in thought. "I prefer to be around others, most of my type like the solitude of nature and are solo unless mated."

A look of disgust marred Kai's face prompting me to raise an eyebrow in her direction.

"How despicable and weak." Was her reply.

That was unexpected coming from my normally compassionate and kind friend. I couldn't get the shocked expression to dissipate. She continued to look at him far longer than warranted and I couldn't help but wonder what possessed my friend to behave in this manner. But before I could inquire further about her behavior Hadeon garnered everyone's attention and started detailing the plan he formulated for our search, shortly followed by the start of our trek into the woods.

Fifteen

CALLUM

It could have been hours or days since Fallon left me here, in charge of an unruly warlock, I couldn't tell anymore. It felt like time was going too slow and too fast simultaneously. My mind is still reeling from everything that has happened. I knew when we were growing up that Fallon had a crush on Finley. It never occurred to me that it went beyond a childish infatuation. I thought his feelings ended when she and I got together—not. Even so, what was witnessed today was very different from that of a crush, it was an obsession, it was madness. How did he see that situation playing out? Surely, he couldn't have thought he could tell Finley what to do, alpha or not, Finley has always done as she desires. He should have known he couldn't bully her into something she didn't want to partake in.

"Could you please stop that? You're interrupting my beauty sleep."

My eyes darted to the warlock. I might have been too lost in thought to remember he was in the room. But my incessant pacing was disturbing him. Good. If I had to be awake with my mind wandering in circles, so should he. He's partly why I'm in this mess.

"I wouldn't want you to get too comfortable, so I think I shall continue."

He eyed me in annoyance, with a huff he closed his eyes and leaned his head back against the chair. It couldn't be comfortable enough to adequately rest in, the chair was quite small compared to him.

He released a resigned sigh before saying, "This won't end well. I'm playing nice for now, to give Finley a head start for retribution because my girl can handle herself. But just know that things will go quite poorly for your brother, especially if he continues his delusional ideas of trying to steal my mate. She will never be his."

Internally I was groaning. I didn't want to talk about my stupid brother. This warlock, whether he was her mate or not, didn't need to convince me about the imminent demise of Fallon's scheming. There wasn't a chance that Finley would ever willingly agree, not after the stunt he tried to pull. The animosity between them had already been high in the last few years. I wasn't sure what happened to their friendship, but I knew it fell apart at some point after our relationship imploded, leaving us all bleeding out.

"Look, I'm only here because my alpha told me to be here, watching you. Otherwise, I wouldn't be involving myself. I make it a principle of mine to stay out of anything involving Finley. I'm not wanted in her life anymore, understandably. I've caused enough setbacks for her over the years, and I atone for that in my way by keeping out of her life and business."

My wandering thoughts started again. Thoughts of us swirling inside my mind, like a montage of all the good and bad we've been through. So many good memories are now tainted by the destructive and heartbreaking ending. Generally, I make it a point to not be a sensitive fucker, but tears pricked unbidden at my eyes, I turned sharply away from the warlock to hide them from showing. The next time he spoke, I knew that I was too slow to avoid his notice.

"While I'm glad you are no longer with Finley, I wish she didn't have to go through the heartbreak she experienced from your actions. But I do wonder about it. Despite how I wish she never had strong feelings for anyone, I do know she loved you greatly, and it sounded like you both were really happy together before she discovered your infidelity. Why did you pursue others? Why destroy what you had?"

Normally when someone would ask me about the past, I would disregard their curiosity but if he was truly her Fates blessed mate, he would be the one loving and caring for her for the rest of her life. Maybe that is what compelled me to contemplate a reply rather than give some shitty nonresponse.

I stopped my pacing and plopped down into the chair across the room from him. I thought about how to respond while I got comfortable for us to have this talk. My elbows rested on my knees, head leaning down, meticulously studying the floor before raising my eyes to survey the warlock.

He contrasted Finley in many ways. He was tall while she was short. He was goldenly tan while she was pale. He had eyes the color of whisky while hers were the green of a spring day. He had a body of toned muscles while she had beautiful curves. They were so different, yet when I looked at him, I could almost imagine them together. They would complement each other nicely despite their differences, or maybe because of it. His personality seems hard, confident, and somewhat abrasive–I'm unsure how much of that is from the situation and how much is normal for him; Finley is bubbly, happy, kind, and strong. He looked like the perfect counterpart for her heart.

It's harder to figure out a response to his question than I thought it would be. It should be easy to pinpoint where my life started falling apart, where I strayed from the path, I outlined for myself, and how I could betray the love of my life for nameless passersby. He must think I am either not going to reply or that I'm taking too long because after a few minutes of me considering how to respond he changes the question to, "Did you ever actually love her?"

The air feels punched out of my lungs at the question. The idea that someone could think I never really loved her makes me feel violently ill. I've loved Finley for a large portion of my life, and still do, I've just never been good at showing it. She has little faith in our past, I can't blame her, my actions would have ruined any confidence she would have had about my love for her.

When I finally feel like I can catch my breath again I respond, "Yes. I've loved Finley since we were children. I loved her when she was mine. I still love her even though I lost her."

My eyes sting even more than they did before. Tears are welling in the corner despite my effort at suppressing my emotions. My inner wolf is whimpering inside, thinking of the loss I caused for us. Throwing myself out of the chair, I walk toward the window and stare outside for a couple minutes trying to recover from the emotional storm that is raging inside of me.

"The thing about Finley and I is that I was never good enough for her. She is like rays of the sun breaking through clouds after a storm and I'm like the fog on a dreary day."

Releasing a sigh, I try to continue the best I can to get this off my chest.

"We were great when we were together. But when we were both in separate colleges we didn't spend as much time together. The more time we spent apart the more I realized she was so much better off without me. I was inadequate to love her, I knew it, she just didn't realize it yet. She was thriving and I was just surviving. When I would think about our future together it was obvious to me that I would be a nuisance to her, holding her back. Once I figured out, I wasn't good enough for her there was this constant heavy weight in the pit of my stomach. It made me start to push her away so I could try to ignore it. I would party and attempt to drown myself in pleasure so I would feel less miserable. What I did, was never about Finley, it was about me. I was selfish. Instead of trying to be a better male for her, someone she could be proud of, I tried to avoid the reckoning that I felt was inevitable."

Sixteen

FINLEY

I've never been told much of Hadeon's history, for all I know the vampire could be positively ancient, while only appearing in his thirties. The thing I do know though is that Xan trusts him and out of the rag-tag group we assembled, he is the one who jumped in and took the point as our impromptu leader.

We went over the plan that Hadeon came up with and by the time he was finished the sun was setting. This is when he wanted us to start our search. The thought was that the lower lighting would help us stay hidden for as long as possible.

When darkness comes upon us, most of us will still be able to see fine. Kai and I have the wolf sight that will help us to see at night like the predators we are. Vampires and squatches are both also adept at night vision. Ry and Leora will be the only ones in our group who will find it more difficult to see, especially since we decided to forgo flashlights since we do not want to draw any unnecessary attention to ourselves. Our solution to this issue was to put them toward the middle of our group while we wandered the woods.

Hadeon insisted on taking the lead which worked out well because his vampire senses are more tuned into our surroundings than anyone else's. We let Ry and Leora follow behind him. Kai insisted on staying close to me and we are trailing them so that if they start to fall too far back, we can herd them in the correct direction. Al insisted on taking up the rear. He said since he is the biggest, he will happily protect us from any potential attacks if someone tries to sneak up on us.

Al being behind us seems to be worsening Kai's already miserable mood. She's honestly been kind of a bitch to him, and I can't figure out why. Al is a little quirky, but he is a nice guy. Kai usually is pretty mellow around people, and I've never seen her treat someone the way she is treating Al—like he is unworthy of basking in her presence. It's a little uncomfortable having to be a constant buffer between these two while also worrying about Xan.

"Keep up *nature boy*." Kai snorts at her sarcastic remark, I'm sure she is trying to insult him since he is a squatch who is allergic to so much and generally adverse to being in nature. I shoot her a narrow-eyed look and elbow her in the ribs. My meaning is clear, knock it off.

"So original, *wolf*. Just remember whatever you throw at me anything you say will probably be something I've heard before. I'm used to people giving me shit about my issues with nature. So do your worst."

I've been trying to be good and ignore them taunting each other but an irritated huff escapes my lips against my restraint. Like I need him tempting her to keep egging him on.

Grabbing Kai's arm, I pull her forward at a quicker pace than we have been walking, trying to gain some space between us and Al. When we are far enough away to be out of direct hearing, I cross my arms and spit out, "What is your problem? Why are you trying to provoke a fight with Al?"

"I just can't stand him!" She yells back.

"Well chill the fuck out, he's a nice guy. We have more important things to worry about than you hating on him for no apparent reason."

She must understand the no-bullshit attitude I'm throwing her way because she takes a deep breath and replies, "Fine, I'm sorry. I'll be good if he'll good." She almost looks pained from agreeing to behave.

As we walked deeper into the forest it appeared that both Kai and Al decided to keep the tentative peace.

Seventeen

XAN

Standing near the window, looking out into the tree-covered forest, the sky was darkening as night began. I will admit that at first being trapped in this cabin with Callum was angering, and my only desire was to cause him frustration. But as time passed with us stuck here together, I realized he wasn't as awful of a man as I originally assumed. He hurt Finley, and for that, I would never like him, but he also wasn't an evil psychopath like his younger brother, Fallon. But at the same time, if he never would have done what he did to her, she would have married him. Meaning, my mate would be married. The thought of that made me feel violent so I just had to be thankful that he was an asshole in the past.

A knock on the door seemed to rouse Callum from the chair he was sitting in. He got up and went to the door, slowly pulling it open only about an inch to see who was there. I assume he wasn't planning on having any visitors or else he wouldn't be so cautious about answering the door.

Surprisingly, when he pulled open the door further to allow the caller to enter, it was the youngest MacGregor son, Knox, who strolled into the room carrying a brown paper bag in his arms.

"Man, it was a real pain in the ass trying to sneak away from our brother the tyrant," Knox said as he placed the bag on the small table before walking to the fridge and grabbing three water bottles.

"What are you doing here? And sneaking away—why are you here without Fallon knowing?" Callum looked utterly suspicious of his younger brother as he approached the table where Knox was now pulling items from inside the bag.

"Well, I brought some dinner obviously for you and the wizard." He continued busing himself pulling out the food. The containers being placed on the table appeared to be Chinese food takeout. Where he got Chinese food out here in the middle of nowhere would most likely forever remain a mystery. But all the same, I was thankful for the forethought to bring food, I was fucking starving, and my stomach chose that moment to rumble loudly.

"Not a wizard," I corrected him.

"Whatever," he huffed in an irritated way. "Get over here and eat before there is nothing left." His hand flung out gesturing to an empty chair at the table.

Cautiously I approached the table and took the empty seat. The aroma wafting from the container of food placed in front of me was so intoxicating that my mouth started to water, drool pooling in my mouth. Damn, either this food was going to be delicious, or I was just that hungry.

Opening the small box revealed the contents to be sweet and sour chicken with steamed rice. I would have much preferred fried rice, but beggars couldn't be choosy, or so they say.

Stuffing his mouth full of chicken, Knox jabbed his fork in my direction before addressing Callum. "What're we going to do about the situation with this guy?"

"What do you mean what are we going to do? Nothing. We are going to do as we are bid."

"That's it? You're just going to listen to Fallon, go along with his outlandish plans?" The anger was evident in Knox's voice. His fork clattered to his plate when he was speaking. He seemed generally surprised by Callum's planned inaction.

"What the hell would we do about it? There's nothing we can do! You know as well as I do that Fallon won the alpha challenge. We can't go against him, not unless we plan to leave the pack." He seemed agitated about having to explain this to Knox.

"That's a cowardly thing to do. This isn't right and you know it. We can't stand by and do nothing. He's losing his freaking mind. We need to do something," he implored Callum.

Callum shoved back from the table; his food being forgotten in the heat of the argument. "Well, what do you suggest? We need to make a plan."

Eighteen

FINLEY

H adeon who had been leading the charge on this mission through the woods, suddenly came to a stop up ahead. He pulled a small, folded paper map from his back pocket and extended it to survey our estimated location.

"Okay, we should be almost there, I think it is just a little further. If I have our location right, there should be a clearing just past these trees and then the cabin should be there." He sounded so confident in his statement, hopefully, he was right. Kai had listened earlier when I told her to stop acting like a bitch to Al, but there truly was no telling how long they would get along. Plus, I was ready to have Xan back and know he was safe and unharmed.

Our group shoved branches and other obtrusive plants out of our way as we pushed toward the edge of the tree line. A vine that was trailing down from one of the trees caught on my skin as I moved it away and scratched me, leaving a small trickle of blood dripping from me. Great. Hopefully, I don't end up getting the blood on my clothing.

I heard Hadeon shout and take off running. What the hell, what happened to us trying to be stealthy and surprising our enemies? He had given a lecture about it after all the arguing earlier. His stern tone brooks no room for interpretation of his demands. So, it was surprising and seemed like something must be happening if he ditched his command.

The rest of us started sprinting to catch up and see what was happening. As soon as I was free of the trees and standing in the clearing, I saw what he had. There halfway between us and the cabin stood three figures in the darkness.

Hadeon rushed at them with extra quick vampire speed and in an instant punches were being exchanged between him and one of the figures. But before any real damage had been caused, I heard a voice that made me sprint faster. Xan yelled out, "Hadeon, stop! It's okay. Stop."

Everything else seemed to go still at the sound of his voice reaching out in the night. Thankfulness flooded me, he was okay. That fact almost had me stumbling on my way to him.

I was almost to Xan when I was close enough to take notice of who the other two people were. A vicious growl ripped out of me at the sight of Callum and Knox. It wasn't often that shifters would growl in human form, but I was angry enough that it came out. I went to lunge at them but before I could get my feet off the ground strong arms wrapped around me, holding me back. It took a second before the scent of Xan was recognizable in my haze of anger, finally knowing it was him holding me back from attacking I ceased my thrashing.

He kept holding me like that, preventing me from acting against the MacGregor brothers as he started speaking to our group. "They are on our side. They decided that Fallon has gone too far off the deep end, and they want to help us."

I scoffed. *Sure, they're just going to go against their alpha brother*, I thought sarcastically to myself. Seeming to notice my disbelief Callum addressed us, "It's true. Fallon has been acting very irrationally and it's against the best interest of the pack. He is creating damage that won't easily be fixed. We want no part of his scheming and attacks. We want to help right his wrongs and prevent further misdeeds. We understand that it means we will most likely need to leave or be exiled from the pack, we are willing to accept that."

"He speaks the truth," Xan spoke, "we just got done eating some dinner and they were releasing me."

Hadeon seemed to accept what was being said quicker than the rest of us, turning to assess the three of them, he said, "Well I guess this problem is resolved."

I was completely stunned by his quick acceptance, I still wanted retribution, but it seemed like I wouldn't be getting any, well at least not yet.

Xan finally let me move enough that I turned to face him and before he could say anything else I threw myself at him, witnesses be damned. He caught me as if he was expecting the action and we were a mess of motion as our lips crashed together, hands weaving into each other's hair, gripping tight with wild abandon.

It was hard to admit it to myself, but I had been scared of what condition he would be in when we found him. I had been so worried he would be hurt or worse—dead. The relief of him being safe and unharmed washed over me like a tidal wave of adrenaline. Uninhibited by the presence of the others I brought my leg up to wrap around Xan's hip and he lifted me at which point I wrapped the other leg around him as well. We were fully entangled in each other, still kissing fiercely when a throat cleared behind us.

Disappointingly, Xan seeming to come to his senses faster than I had, pulled back, ending the kiss. Our chests were heaving hard and fast as he turned us so that we both could comfortably look at our friends and potential temporary allies without disengaging from each other.

"While we are all glad to have recovered Xan, we probably should head out before anyone else comes back and finds out Callum and Knox let him go. Where to?" Hadeon asked as he looked at Xan.

"Remember the Wimbleton estate?"

Hadeon's eyebrows raised, "Yes."

"It's been a while since I was there last, but we can all stay there temporarily while we figure things out and make plans for what comes next."

Hadeon agreed with Xan's plan to stay at this place that I knew nothing about. I had lots of questions about it but now wasn't the time.

Knox had a car here but the two vehicles the rest of us came in were still parked where we left them, and there wasn't room for all of us in Knox's car, so we agreed that Xan and I would be the ones to walk back through the woods and collect the cars. Once we got the cars collected, we would each drive one to wherever the Wimbleton estate.

When the others drove away, Hadeon riding shotgun to give directions, we started walking toward the woods. We were about halfway to the cars when Xan stopped walking and turned in my direction. He came to me, and our kiss started again, with just as much intensity as earlier, if not more.

"I was always going to come back to you," Xan whispered to me.

I looked at him with questioning brows before he continued to explain to me that when everything was going down with Fallon and his cronies, he stashed some ingredients for spell work so he could escape and had just been waiting to be left unattended to be able to use them.

He suddenly had a mischievous expression take over his facial features as he reached into his pocket. He pulled out a handful of something and tossed it at me while murmuring some words too low for me to make clear what he was saying.

Between one blink and the next vines crawled from the tree behind me and wrapped around my wrists, pulling them tightly towards the sky and holding them there.

He smirked as he stood back surveying the situation, he put me in while wetness pooled between my legs.

He prowled closer to me and ran his nose along my neck, seeming to be intentionally teasing. Using his foot, he pushed my legs to be wider before divesting me of my pants.

So now here I stand, secured to a tree, only my top half covered. I'm sure my face would be flaming with embarrassment if we weren't alone in the desolate woods. I wonder if this was his plan the whole time, maybe that's why it was us collecting the cars rather than heading to our meet point with the others. I have no complaints about the way things are turning out.

He started working his zipper down on his pants, then stroking slowly on his cock from base to tip. My hands twitched in their bindings, wishing to be able to reach out and touch him. I couldn't help it, the desire to be the one touching his shaft had me squirming against the tree, trying futilely to release my hands.

"Stop teasing me," I commanded him, starting to be frustrated by how badly I wanted his cock inside of me.

He chuckled before ultimately closing the distance and taking action. The tip of his cock pushed against my entrance, too gently at first before pushing harder and entering.

We both groaned when he bottomed out inside me and started a rhythm of thrusting in and out. The sensation of his movements was delicious. I was relieved that this was happening now, I wouldn't have been able to make it however far to somewhere else to be able to connect with him like this.

He shifted my leg up higher to be able to get deeper inside me, hitting the most sensitive place while trailing sloppy kisses on my neck. I was starting to unravel with all the different delightful sensations coexisting together.

"I missed you, mate." He whispered before peppering a kiss behind my ear.

Stars burst behind my eyes which closed on their own as I came completely undone at his words. My orgasm exploded out of me. Tingles erupted all over my body.

"Mate?" I panted after my wits came back.

He grunted as he stilled, exploding inside me as he found his release as well.

"Yes, you are my fate-blessed mate."

At that moment I realized, nothing had ever felt truer.

Nineteen

FINLEY

Once we had righted ourselves, Xan and I split up, each taking a set of keys and driving the abandoned vehicles. I had to pay extra attention driving since I didn't know where we were going—Wimbleton Estate. I followed close behind Xan as he drove in the direction that would take us back toward our town of Silver Ridge.

When we got close to the exit to town, Xan turned off onto a side road. From there we had a couple more turns that led us to a dirt road which was rough and jostled me with every bump I passed. When we got to the end, I realized this dirt road was a crude driveway to a house. The front of the yard was surrounded by a ten-foot black iron fence that had sharp points all along the top. Up above the gate entrance was the name of the property, some of the letters appeared loose and were slightly wobbling in the breeze.

The gates swung open as we approached without anyone opening them, and from the looks of them they were not automated. This led me to believe that Xan was the one responsible for that.

We pulled up close to the home and as I turned off the vehicle, I stared up at the opposing structure standing in front of me. It was a black-colored Victorian-style home, that I would guess was built in the late 1700s based on my obsession with architecture and hobby of browsing listings for older homes. This house while probably beautiful back in its beginning, had certainly seen better days. The structure was nice and straight, sturdy looking from what was visible on quick inspection, but the paint was peeling throughout the exterior.

Xan approached where I stood and quietly watched me as I assessed the building. "Welcome to my home away from home," he said.

"You own this place?" I was generally surprised by the revelation seeing as I knew how much he loved the apartment above the nightclub in which he lived.

"Yes, I bought Wimbleton Estate in my early 20s after I started making decent money selling hexes and spells online. I was able to purchase it for a deal, mostly because it needs significant work, but I might have also relied a teensy bit on magic to help with the price." He gave a wry grin at the admission of his underhanded deeds.

I couldn't help the snort that fell from my mouth. It sounded exactly like something he would do, so I couldn't say I was surprised in the least.

The house truly would be a sight if it were ever fixed up. I wonder if Xan has plans to do so in the future. From the windows on this side of the house, you could tell that it was at least a three-level house. The lower-level windows were those large ones that had to be at least eight feet tall, maybe more. The unique thing was that it had a turret on one side. I always thought older homes with terrets were very interesting, but I had never seen one in real life only in photos online.

"Come on, the others are surely here by now and waiting for us. We need to meet up with everyone and get settled in." He ushered me up the large steps of the wrap-around porch and in through the tall double doors that were equipped with creepy lion-faced brass door knockers.

The interior that was exposed when he opened the right door and we entered, was in the same dilapidated state. While it didn't necessarily look unsafe it was in desperate need of at minimum cosmetic repairs. There were several rooms visible from the entryway and each had various shades of paint on the walls with no rhyme or reason and were incomplete, some rooms had more than one color on each wall. It made me wonder if this was something the previous owner did before selling to Xan, or what.

He led me through a series of rooms until we came to a tall bookcase that went from floor to ceiling. As he approached Xan threw out his hand and a book slid forward on the bottom shelf with an accompanying click that caused the bookcase to swing outward, revealing a room. Not just any room—a library room that has shelves floor to ceiling on every wall. There were multiple couches in the center of the room and there our friends—and reluctant allies—waited for us, some with glasses of amber liquid in hand.

"Ah, you're finally here!" Kai yelled exasperatedly as she approached me and I tossed her keys toward her, which she skillfully caught. "What took so long?" She asked as she crossed her arms and gave us an assessing look. She must have figured it out because she smirked before following up with a, "Oh, I get it." Snickering to herself before heralding me further into the room.

The others seemed to quickly figure out what Kai already interpreted, and no one seemed to have any input about it but there was a low growl that was admitted from the direction in which Callum was sitting. Fuck him. He had no right to be upset about anything involving me, he hadn't been in years. I let his grouching roll off me, leaving me unaffected.

Xan strode forward and clasped hands with Hadeon and thanked him for leading the charge to rescue him, despite it being unnecessary. He then went on to give Ry a pat on the shoulder as well as offer a chaste kiss on Leora's cheek. The kiss didn't cause any jealousy in me, I knew that Leora had been a part of his life for a long time, as well as feeling secure in the fact that Xan was right—we were mates. Lastly, he offered a small nod in the direction of Callum and Knox before taking a seat on one of the couches.

He beckoned me to sit with him and as I went to sit down, he grabbed me and hauled me onto his lap where he settled his arm securely around my waist.

He has always been very affectionate to me since we got together but I think that being away from me and worrying about what could've been happening drove him to be extra touchy-feely.

"Welcome to the Wimbleton Estate. I own this home. There are seven bedrooms, most situated on the top two floors. There are five bathrooms in total, two on this level, one on the second, and two on the top. The property has fifty acres, so if you go outside the fence at the back of the house you may access the woodlands, which would be great for running if any of you shifters are interested. This place has for the most part been sitting empty while I have been working to get it rehabbed—which has been a slow process since it was never a time-sensitive priority until now. While I own the home, it is registered under a fictitious name that I occasionally use to keep my anonymity. That being said, that means the only people who know of my ownership are in this room, so no one will find us unless we want them to."

Everyone nodded keeping up with his introduction. There were seven rooms and nine of us. The mated pairs would share rooms, the rest getting rooms to themselves. Xan led us all out of the room and started assigning rooms to each guest. On the second floor, he turned and looked at Hadeon. No words were exchanged but it was clear there was a silent understanding when he told Callum and Knox that they would be sharing that room. Hadeon didn't need any instruction from Xan, he walked directly to the room next door, opening the door, and walking into it without another word.

Once everyone else had a room to settle into, Xan took me to the last remaining door on the third floor and this was the room we would inhabit. It appeared to be the master bedroom as well as the room that had access to the turret. I couldn't help but to go to the windows of the terret and stare out in awe.

Xan approached me from behind, wrapping his arms around me. With his mouth running along my neck he rasped out, "Finally we're alone. Thank fuck."

I mentally mirrored that sentiment, alone thank fuck. He made me relive that thankfulness over and over that night.

Twenty

FINLEY

When I fell asleep it was not a soft lulling, it was crashing, sleeping like the dead. I probably didn't start out dreaming, but now I was having the most wonderful dream. It was the most euphoria I remember feeling from slumber. I was warm and cozy in the large soft bed in the master bedroom of Wimbleton Estate, where I fell asleep next to Xan, my mate. *Mate,* it's something I never gave much thought to in my life, but now that I had Xan, I felt more complete than I had in my entire existence. But that's what fate-blessed mates were, the missing piece of your soul, so it made sense to feel this way now that I knew what we were.

I started feeling even warmer, feeling heat spread up my body, seeming to radiate out from my core. Then slowly I realized I wasn't dreaming after all. I had thought I was still sleeping because of how much pleasure I was experiencing, but no I was awake, and as I opened my eyes, I saw the cause of that feeling.

The light that was streaming through the turret windows—which were not curtained—illuminated caramel-brown eyes glowing from between my legs as they met mine. Xan held that eye contact while continuing his ministrations, licking and sucking on my clit.

It wasn't long before I started wiggling, writhing, feeling close, but needing *more.* When I said as much, he rubbed two fingers against my entrance, gathering the wetness on his fingers before they thrust into me. With expert precision, he worked my G-spot putting the perfect amount of pressure. I was almost there and then he changed from licking to sucking *hard,* and there was no holding back the orgasm that exploded out of me. It happened fast and I had no time to prepare myself to stifle any sounds that flew from my parted lips.

My cheeks heated at the possibility that anyone else heard us. The idea of being heard probably should have felt more shameful than it did, but I also kind of secretly enjoyed that debauched idea.

Xan placed an open-mouthed kiss on my clit before pulling himself away from me and starting to head toward the door.

"What are you doing?" My confusion was clear in my voice.

"Well, I was eating my *breakfast,* and now I have a few things to go take care of. Mainly checking in with Hadeon about the MacGregors staying with us." He shrugged his shoulder as if he was unaffected by everything that just took place.

It took me a minute to get out of the haze his words created, he was too good at talking dirty to me, and I loved every minute of it. But then I registered what he was referencing.

"That's why Hadeon is in the room next to theirs? You wanted him to keep his eye on them and report back to you if there was anything suspicious?"

He nodded solemnly. "For starters, I don't particularly like them. But also, just because they say they are willing to forsake their pack and family doesn't mean I believe them yet. At some point maybe I will get there, but for now, Hadeon will keep an eye on them. Having a best friend who is a vamp who has his history comes in handy. He understood what I wanted him to do without me even having to ask him."

I threw off the silky cover of the blanket and slid from the bed. If Xan—who wasn't much of a morning person—was awake and out of bed, the others probably were as well. Hence, it was time for me to get moving too. We were going to need to have a group meeting today and go over what ideas we all had for taking care of our asshole Fallon problem.

He was staring salaciously at my naked body as I walked toward him. When I was standing in front of him, I kissed him, wrapping my arms tightly around the back of his neck.

We were lost in the kiss for a minute. But when I tried to drag him back toward the bed, he broke the kiss and let me know that as much as he would love to stay there with me all day things needed to be done. Pouting at him I let him know I understood, but thoroughly didn't like it.

"There is something I want," I whispered to him, kissing the underside of his jaw.

"And what's that?" His rough voice showed just how not unaffected he was.

"Do you know what shifters do with their mates?" I asked him.

He seemed to think about it for a minute and followed up with, "No, I don't know a whole lot about the culture of mating for shifters. What is it?"

A wicked grin spread across my face before I could rein it in. I let my teeth scrape gently over the skin of his neck before answering him. "Well shifters bite their mates with their fangs, to mark them, it shows ownership. Not in a way that is demeaning as if the other person is property, but it is done to show others that person belongs to someone. Mates bite and mark each other when they have accepted that connection."

His eyes burned bright as he assessed me silently. "And you want to mark me?"

I groaned unintentionally. "Yes, desperately. I want to sink my fangs into you right here." I said to him as I placed my mouth loosely on the junction between his neck and shoulder. My mouth salivating at the thought of driving my teeth deep into his flesh. "But I don't know anyone else who is mated to someone who isn't a shifter, so I don't know a whole lot about it. I feel like I shouldn't do it since you can't bite me back—well not in the same way." I said to him with a pout evident on my face.

He seemed to be thinking for a minute before he smiled broadly. "I think I have an idea of how we could make it work."

I straightened at that. Excitement rushed through me. "How?"

"Leave the details to me to work out. But I think I know how we can *both* mark each other and trust me the idea is as thrilling to me as it seems to be to you." With that he gave me another quick kiss before telling me to get dressed and heading out the door, saying to meet him downstairs when I was ready.

Twenty-One

FINLEY

I took a quick shower in the bathroom across the hall to try and make myself feel more awake. Instead of using a boiling temperature like I normally would for showers or baths, I used a very mild temperature hoping the shock to my system would help. Unfortunately, I didn't feel any more awake at the end, so all I did was make myself uncomfortable for those handfuls of minutes.

Yanking open the shower curtain, with more force than necessary—which was most likely due to feeling unfulfilled after not getting to take a ride on Xan's cock like I wanted—I noticed that there was a small bundle of clothing sitting on the countertop. There hadn't been any sounds of anyone entering and leaving the clothes, so I knew instinctively that Xan was the one responsible for leaving them, and seeing as I had no clothes since my house was burned to a crisp along with all my belongings, I knew magic was probably involved with their acquisition.

I unfolded the bundle and saw he had left me a pair of loose-fitting athletic shorts with a racerback-style tank top. No underwear or bra, obviously intentional. After shaking my head at his audacity I got dressed, pleasantly surprised that everything fit to perfection.

When I exited the bathroom, I took a look around the hallway and saw no sign of him, so I decided to head downstairs to see where everyone was.

By the time I made it to the bottom of the lower level, I was panting slightly with the excursion it took to climb down all those stairs. I was in great cardio shape, as I often ran in my wolf form for long periods, so I was a little annoyed by being winded now.

I used my excellent hearing to listen to the sounds of our group. Hearing noise coming from the direction of the kitchen I headed there.

Upon walking into the room all the talking ceased momentarily before Kai smirked at me. She asked, "Did you get any actual sleep last night? Or were you too *busy*?"

Despite that momentary enjoyment earlier about the idea of being overheard embarrassment heated my cheeks now. Oh, I was going to kill her. The satisfied grin she gave me let me know she interpreted as much from my facial expression.

When I lunged in her direction—not to kill her—she threw a handful of dry cereal in my direction like mini torpedoes.

We both broke out laughing, not long later and the others in the room also broke out in laughter as well. When we finally stopped horsing around, I looked around the room to survey who was there. Other than Kai and me, everyone was here except for Xan and Callum. It made me nervous that those two were the only ones missing, it made me worried they were together somewhere. That could potentially be a dangerous situation.

I tried my best not to worry about it, trying to trust in the fact that Callum allegedly wanted to be on our side of this fight. But my brain kept having this niggling thought about Xan not liking Callum and worrying about them getting into a confrontation. We didn't need our group to be divided. If we wanted to take down Fallon, we were going to need everyone on our side that we could manage to get.

Just when my worry was starting to crest the highest both the subjects of my thoughts entered the kitchen—together. I intently looked them both over, trying to assess if there were any injuries to either of them. They both appeared to be fine. So, it seemed as if they weren't fighting. I guess that is good news.

Chewing my breakfast, I watched Xan get everyone's attention. "Callum is going to be making some calls today to see who from Fang can be swayed to join us in our stance against Fallon."

Callum spoke up, "I have a few ideas of potential allies I'll contact today and when we regroup this afternoon, I can let you know how it panned out."

"Knox, your brother said you might be able to access maps for your family's property and blueprints for the main house?" Xan asked.

Knox gave him confirmation of this. He said he had a friend who owed him a favor and would be able to get them blown up to a readable size and printed. He would reach out to his friend and pick up the plans today.

Hadeon would be collecting intel on Fallon to see what he has been up to since we last saw him.

Leora and Ry—being people the pack was unfamiliar with—would go into town to collect some supplies for our time here. They made a list of items to pick up including some clothing for everyone, food, and other needed supplies.

Xan asked Kai and Al about helping clean up the estate today since we would be staying here for an indeterminate amount of time. Of course, they both agreed, more than willing to lend a hand, but immediately started arguing over who would handle what. I noticed for the most part it was Kai instigating the disagreement. Al would offer an area in which he would start his cleaning, then Kai would tell him why that wouldn't work. I shook my head at her antics.

One of these days I would find out why she was always being such a stinker anytime she had to interact with Al. But today was not going to be that day because Xan told them, "Work it out between yourselves, I need to steal Finley for a minute, and we will be busy so don't come looking for us."

He grabbed my hand and hauled me from the room at a fast pace. As the door swung shut behind us, Kai stopped arguing long enough for me to hear her say, "I'm sure you will be busy." Followed by her signature loud laughter.

Twenty-Two

FINLEY

We kept up a fast pace as Xan led me to this mystery location for his unknown purpose. I asked multiple times in the last couple of minutes what was happening, but he was keeping a tight lid on his plans. I even tried being a little pouty like a brat and it got me nowhere. All I knew was that it must have been something important because we were practically racing to the destination.

After several turns, we reached a door and when we stepped outside, I deduced it must have been the backdoor. I followed across the yard until we were standing at the entrance to a beautiful black metal and glass conservatory.

I stood still for a minute looking at it with amazement. I've always thought these old conservatories were so cool. This house truly had everything I could have ever wanted in a dream house. I quickly fell in love with this place. If we weren't staying here because of our current shitty situation, I would happily stay here long-term.

With an ominous creak, the door was pried open, and we were entering. I wasn't sure what to expect to find inside but it wasn't what I found. There were plants in more varieties than I'd even know the names of, and they were alive, something I didn't expect to see at an estate where no one had been living.

"How?" I asked as I turned to look at Xan while gesturing toward all the greenery that surrounded us.

"I haven't lived here until now, but this is where I grow all my ingredients for my spells and potions. I figured out a couple of years ago that it was cheaper for me to grow all the plants instead of ordering from someone else. Also, it was starting to be a little suspicious—the number of items—that I was ordering. I didn't want to raise any flags ordering tons of herbs and plants when on paper my only busy is a nightclub."

I could easily understand what he meant about it looking suspicious and it made sense to grow the plants if he wanted to keep his other business under wraps from authorities. It was lucky that he had the gardening know-how. I don't think I would have been able to do the same if the roles were reversed. Despite my desire to grow plants at the house I owned everything always died too easily, I was just very bad at growing things, I guess. But Xan, like many other warlocks and witches, had an affinity for gardening as proven by my current surroundings.

He took me around the conservatory giving me a tour of the place. He had plants and herbs to fill pretty much any need. I noticed that the largest section of plants was reserved for poisonous and toxic species. I didn't know what I was looking at until I reached out with the intent to touch a plant and was stopped by a swift push of Xan's arm knocking mine away—not to hurt but to protect.

Luckily, I hadn't touched my fingers to the plant yet and now I knew better. The good news is that in the future I most likely wouldn't be spending any time unsupervised in here since I did not need it. I still appreciated him sharing a place that meant so much to him with me.

Once he was done showing me the different sections, he told me to wait there, and he ran off into the labyrinth of plant life to grab some supplies he said he needed to fulfill our mysterious purpose of being here.

After a couple of minutes of being separated, he popped back into sight, and I followed him to a section in the back where there was some comfortable outdoor furniture.

Sitting on a semi-comfortable couch I watched in silence as he took various ingredients into a mortar that he must have had stored somewhere around here. When he added everything, he needed he took a pestle and started grinding the mixture up while chanting at too low a volume for me to determine the words he was saying.

When it was done the mix in the bowl looked disgusting. But I imagine that is how a lot of magical objects looked.

He sat down on the couch across from me and beckoned me to him. I approached and when I went to sit on the couch, he shook his head no and demanded I sit in his lap instead.

Straddling his lap, I sat face-to-face with him. He stuck his finger into the goop he created and smeared some on my neck then asked me to do the same on his neck.

I didn't know what this was or what it was for I curiously did as bid, and I placed the disgusting stuff on his skin in the same place he put mine—the place shifters mark their mates.

"After you told me earlier about your desire to mark me, I had an idea that could work for it to be able to be reciprocated?"

"You mean you might have a way to mark me as well?" I asked tilting my head in a please explain motion.

"If I'm right, a mirroring spell might be able to help create a mark on you." Then he continued to explain how it worked. When I bit him, I needed to bite where the paste was now on his neck. With the mirroring spell in place, I would also receive a bite mark on my skin where the stuff is on my neck.

Excitement buzzed under my skin at the prospect of proudly being able to display a mating mark for the world to see. One thing concerned me though. "Is that goop going to taste disgusting when I bite you?"

He barked out a laugh. "Probably. But I think this is going to work."

"Do you know when it is that a mate produces a claiming mark?" Raising my eyebrows, I asked him. He didn't know the other part so I figured I might have to explain. I was correct in the assumption and went on to explain that the claiming bites were given during intercourse with their partner.

Seeing as he had no qualms with that, we ended up making love there in the conservatory surrounded by plants, and right as I was reaching my peak of ecstasy, I sharpened my teeth and sunk my fangs into his muscular neck. I thought it would be kind of nasty to do because of the magic on his neck and the blood I was sure I would taste on my tongue. But all I could feel was pure contentment at the moment. No bad tastes registered. As I pulled my teeth out of his skin I briefly wondered if the spell worked but that was quickly confirmed when I felt a stinging pain suddenly radiate from the same spot on my neck. At that moment of my mark being forged, Xan came with a shout and we both went still, panting, wrapped up in each other.

Twenty-Three

FINLEY

When we were finished claiming each other we left the conservatory and headed back towards the house. It was quickly becoming time to reconvene with our friends to further discuss our problems with Fallon and the Fang pack.

When we entered through the back door of the house no one was directly in sight, so it took a minute to see where they were. Everyone was in the kitchen except Al and Kai. No one paid much attention to us as they were busy unloading bags from the supply run and unrolling maps on the countertop, so I suggested to Xan that we find Al and Kai for the meeting.

I used my strong sense of smell to follow her scent to find my best friend. To say what I found when I located her was unexpected was an understatement. I opened the door to the library room where her scent was the strongest and stood stock still for a minute in complete surprise. The room was a complete mess, unlike the last time I checked in with her. Chaos was the only true way to describe it. Then there were the clear signs that Al and Kai had just been fucking.

They both jumped when I threw open the door. Al had just finished zipping up his jeans. Both quickly looked guilty and Kai—someone who doesn't have any shame when it comes to advertising her personal life—went completely red in the face, blotches building on her neck and cheeks. Her finger pointed threateningly in our direction before gritting out, "Not. One. Single. Word."

She didn't want anyone knowing about what took place here and as flabbergasted as I was from this turn of events, I would give her the privacy she requested until a time in which she was ready to share what happened here.

Not wanting to cause her further distress I shut the door and yelled, "Meet us in the kitchen, everyone wants to strategize!" Before retreating from the vicinity.

When we got far enough away, I couldn't hold it in anymore. I burst out laughing. Xan seemed to be of a similar mindset about our discovery because he let out a booming laugh as well.

"I was worried about them killing each other today when they were supposed to be working together, I guess we misread that situation." He snorted with a headshake.

We spent a few minutes hidden away unable to help ourselves from wrapping back up in each other's arms, lips exploring each other. The thrill of our mating claim settled between us with excitement and passion.

When we reemerged, we headed straight toward the kitchen to join the others. Kai and Al were both already there, standing on opposite sides of the room, both looking uncomfortable and like they were back to 'hating' each other. I knew better now though.

Everyone stopped talking when we entered, and I wasn't sure why at first. A fierce growl came from Callum before he flew from his chair near the island and was standing before me. Grabbing my chin he turned my head, looking at my neck. His fingers skimmed the skin of my neck before he growled out, "What the hell?"

As I jerked away from his touch his hand was removed from my neck, coming away with a small amount of blood on his fingertips.

As a warlock, Xan didn't have any speed-related prowess that a normal human wouldn't have had, but he moved quicker than I thought possible at that moment. He grabbed ahold of Callum's wrist, twisting it to the side. He bared his teeth at Callum, looking downright feral at that moment. "If you plan to live, you will keep your hands off my mate. Touch her again and it will be the last thing you do before death greets you."

I knew since we were going to be allies, I should probably step in and stop Xan from doing anything irrational like killing or maiming, but seeing him angry about Callum's hands on me, was extremely hot. We might have just experienced a blissful coupling, but I could feel myself getting all hot and bothered by his ferocity.

All the shifters in the room seemed to turn to look at me suddenly. Oops, my smell must have changed, broadcasting my debauched thoughts to everyone who had the sensitive noses of shifters. My face heated slightly in chagrin.

Knox seemed to recoup his wits faster than the others and asked, "That looks like a mate-claiming mark. How is that possible with him not being a shifter?"

A smirk crossed Xan's face; I could see a sarcastic comment loading in his brain before he turned toward Knox. Taking his hands, he moved them like forming an invisible rainbow in the air and drawing out the word, "magic."

Knox was annoyed by the answer, but it also was true. Maybe if Xan hadn't paired the answer with his sarcastic tone Knox would have happily accepted the response. Instead, it just ruffled Knox and made him ask again how it was possible.

Xan pinned him with a look but when he saw the curious looks of our other friends, he rolled his eyes before explaining in detail the mirroring spell he created and then showing off his claiming mark on his neck.

Kai high-fived me and gave me a way to go, but Callum stalked out of the room with thumping steps the entire way. We needed to make plans for what was to come, but he made no sign of coming back and when Kai went to look for him and he was nowhere to be found we decided to postpone our prep until tomorrow, waiting one night wouldn't hurt. It was a better idea anyway to let everyone cool off, so we didn't end up with any fights on our hands. So, Leora handed out some clothes and toiletries to those of us still here and we all broke away to head to our respective rooms for the night.

Tomorrow we would regroup, hopefully with less drama, and get to planning the downfall of my ex-best friend.

Twenty-Four

CALLUM

I knew that I truly had no right to feel the irrational anger that I felt when I found out about Finley and Xan's mating. I knew it, and yet, I still felt it, I guess that's why it was called irrational anger.

It had been a long time since she and I had been in a relationship, which had been my fault. But it still felt like losing something, seeing the claim made, one that she would never be able to undo. It felt like something inside of my soul was breaking loose. Like I had pieces of myself breaking apart, free-floating toward space.

I couldn't stay in the room after the discovery had been made. My wolf felt like it was pacing inside my body, causing me to feel even more unsettled. I needed to run, to get away from here, as far as I could. At least for a little while. I needed space and time to process what happened.

Releasing my wolf, I sprinted away from the estate as fast as my four furry legs would take me. It was a terrible idea to leave unnecessarily since we were technically fugitives of the pack and there would be shifters on the hunt for us. I couldn't change my mind though, I continued to run.

□

***

□

I ran for hours last night in my wolf form. It was freeing to let him take the lead for a while, being cautious that no one followed me. Everything was simpler in our wolf bodies. Nothing was ever as complicated as when we were human. As wolves everything was more primal and at our baser level of existence.

When I made it back to the estate it was already the middle of the night. I snuck inside as quietly as possible, but it turned out to be unnecessary since everyone had already gone to bed for the evening.

The house was silent as I trudged up the stairs with mud covering a large portion of my body. When I was running through some woods, I didn't notice the change of ground until I fell into the water of a brown bog. I emerged from the water soaking wet and the area surrounding the water held no grass, it was completely dirt, so that is how I got so covered in mud.

I took a shower, scrubbing off the mess, and trying to let my emotions run down the drain with it, which turned out to be more challenging than just being determined to release those feelings.

When I was clean, and the stink removed from my person I headed to the room I shared with my brother Knox. From the stillness of the room, I figured he would be deep in sleep but when I waltzed into the room he was there, sitting silently on his bed, awake.

He scowled at me when we made eye contact. I knew he was probably pissed at me, if the tables were reversed, I would be thoroughly pissed with him, enough so that I would probably throw a couple of punches. I wouldn't blame him if he felt like he needed to give me a walloping. But he didn't.

He glared at me, arms crossed before demanding in a cool lethal voice, "Where were you?"

I gripped the back of my neck tightly, hoping the pressure would help keep my mood in check before I answered, "I needed to get away for a little while. I went for a run."

The glare he had been giving me didn't lessen any with my answer, if anything it intensified. "That was a bullshit stunt you pulled. It shouldn't be a surprise to you that something like this was coming. We already knew what he told us, about them being mates. It was not news to us. Why did you flip your shit so bad?"

Embarrassment flooded me. I knew he was right. But it didn't change the fact that I still cared for Finley. I kept my distance from her after I broke her heart, it was only fair of me to do. But it didn't make my love for her disappear just because I was a stupid asshole. I loved her from a distance, silently hoping someday maybe I could make it up to her. Prove how wrong I had been about us. Earn her trust and love once again.

I tried my best to explain it to Knox. He nodded along as I fumbled my way through explaining my feelings, dashed hopes, and dreams. The future I hoped for was suddenly blown apart by the arrival of her mate—a connection that would always trump all others.

When I had finished word-vomiting my feelings all over my brother he encouraged me to 'figure my shit out quick' seeing as we would all be living together, allying against our corrupt brother. I knew he was right. I needed to get my head right as soon as possible.

We talked for a long time and when I finally started drifting to sleep the sun was already starting to rise outside. The exhaustion I felt from the run and finally opening up exposing the feelings I had locked up for years drug me down to a restless sleep.

Twenty-Five

FINLEY

Last night was such a clusterfuck. For starters, I was curious about what happened between Kai and Al. She hated him, at least that's the way things appeared before catching them after they were intimate. How did that even come about? Also, it was pretty strange that Kai didn't want to talk about it. She has been my best friend a long time and she never withholds details from me about her conquests—sometimes even when I wish she would. So, her being tightlipped about the situation made me nervous. They were already volatile towards each other before but what they be like now that they slept together?

Then there was the bullshit caused by Callum, I hadn't even thought about the others seeing the evidence of the bite mark on my neck and even if they did, I didn't think it would cause the strife it did. But when he saw the mark and flew off the handle it was unexpected. I don't see how he thinks it is any of his business, I haven't been his business in a long time. He didn't care enough about me toward the end of our relationship to protect me from hurt, and to stay committed to me, so he has no right to have feelings about this. I'm happy—well as happy as I can be until after we deal with his brother.

Callum ran off last night after his tantrum and while I wanted nothing more than to let him fester in whatever hurt he felt, we all knew it could be dangerous for us if someone saw him or if he decided to betray us. With that in mind, we all spent hours trying to call his phone, searching the woods for him, and keeping a lookout on the off chance he decided to lead our enemies to our door.

When the exhaustion of the day became too much, we decided to call it quits on our unfruitful efforts. Hadeon volunteered to keep a lookout as a precaution, so we were not caught unaware. My sleep was fitful at best even wrapped in the arms of my lover, leaving me feeling as if I had no sleep at all.

Slowly, in an attempt not to wake Xan, I lightly grasped his arm and removed it from my waist. When I peeked behind me seeing him still firmly asleep, I silently slipped from the bed, grabbing clothes for the day. Once I was dressed, face washed, and hair secured in a ponytail I went downstairs in search of anyone who might also be awake.

I didn't spot anyone on my way to the kitchen, which was fine. Coffee should always come before the conversation, so I made a cup of coffee and left plenty of space for the decadent creamer that Leora picked up yesterday on the supply run. As I picked up my cup, turning around to head outside, I was met with the unexpected presence of Hadeon. The damn vampire was too quiet for my good, startled I jolted, spilling the hot coffee over the edge, splashing some on my hand holding the mug.

"Shit!" I hissed out as the burn intensified on my skin. I slammed the mug down on the counter. Glaring at Hadeon I said, "What the hell man? Maybe announce yourself once in a while."

With speed too quick for my eyes he was suddenly in front of me. I started to stumble back before he reached out and handed me a hand towel for my coffee mess. The usually stoic Hadeon almost looked chagrin for a moment, "Sorry, I didn't mean to scare you. I heard you down here and figured I would update you."

I took the hand towel from him and started cleaning up the mess, first wiping off my hand and then the puddle on the floor. I raised an eyebrow in his direction, I silently went ahead, waiting impatiently to know what he wanted to tell me.

"Callum came back close to dawn. No others were with him, and no one followed. He was in wolf form until he got back covered in filth. His brother laid into him pretty good when he got back. I can hear them from my room." The statement confirmed what I suspected—that Hadeon was in the room next door to theirs to spy on them. He continued, "It doesn't sound like he got into any trouble. He ran in wolf form, trying to work out his feelings."

I sighed irritated, pinching the bridge of my nose. "Fucker doesn't get to have feelings about this," I grumbled. Hadeon's lip twitched upward on one side in a simile of a smirk before he agreed with me.

Hadeon excused himself to work on planning and I took my coffee outside intending to drink it in quiet on the back porch surrounded by the late morning sun. But when I swung the door shut, turning toward a sitting area I found none other than Callum occupying the space, looking forlorn.

I scowled at him as he looked up at me with probably the saddest expression, I'd ever seen him wear. Plans derailed I turned around to go back inside, not wanting to spend more time than necessary with the man. I might be happily mated now but it didn't change the bitterness I felt from the pain he had caused me in the past.

Hand grasping the doorknob he called out to me before I could twist it to enter the house. "Please wait." His voice was quiet, tinged with the same sadness.

I whipped around to face his direction. "What do you want?" I volleyed the question at him like it was a grenade I could use to blow him to pieces.

"Please sit, I think we need to talk."

"There isn't anything to talk about Callum." I retorted, but before I could turn back to the door again, he was out of his seat and approaching me. I watched him closely, unsure of his intent. When he stood in front of me, he sank to his knees before me, bowing his head to the ground in a show of submission. "Please just stay for a minute, talk to me, let us put the past behind us, move forward." He begged me.

I was half inclined to ignore his pleas and go back inside as I planned but something was stopping me from doing it. I couldn't decipher the exact reason for it, maybe it was seeing him on his knees before me begging, but I found myself crossing the porch and taking a seat at the outdoor table. "Fine, five minutes." With that, he was immediately up and coming to sit with me.

I hoped that I wouldn't regret agreeing to talk with him. I had little interest in having a heart-to-heart, and even less interest in drudging up the painful past.

At first, he just stared at me, seeming surprised that I would stay and talk. When he made no moves to start whatever discussion he had planned I narrowed my eyes before telling him to get on with it.

"I know it is reasonable for you to never forgive me for what I put you through, but I want you to know that I am sorry. Finley, I truly am sorry for what I did, and how things ended between us. I won't make excuses for my behavior, but I will say that I never felt worthy of you, and as it got closer to our marriage that feeling of inferiority kept growing. I was sabotaging myself in an attempt to get you to do what I couldn't leave. I knew I wasn't strong enough to break things off. But I felt it in my bones, that you were not to be mine. I felt on a cellular level that you had something greater waiting for you. But I was too selfish to let go. So, I punished my cowardice and sabotaged rather than manning up and telling you how things felt wrong."

I scoffed before huffing, "You did an excellent job sabotaging. Would it have hurt if you told me how you felt? Yes, I think it would have been devastating, but I think what you did hurt worse. I spent a long time after feeling not good enough. First, I found you with someone else. Then when I went to Fallon, my best friend, the person who was supposed to be there for me unconditionally, he told me it was what I deserved. I lost my fiancé and my best friend all in the same night."

Tears were welling in his eyes from the moment I said what he did was worse. "I truly am sorry Fin. I know I hurt you badly and I can't change that. I also knew Fallon cared for you before we started dating, but I never thought he would be vindictive to you. I underestimated his hatred of us being together, of you choosing me over him. You might not have known it at the time, but that is what he saw it as. He saw it as a betrayal. He loved you and when you 'chose' me he was hurt. I am sorry you lost not just me but him as well." He paused seeming to think for a minute. "My outburst yesterday was wrong. I felt blindsided and I let feelings from the past cloud my judgment."

"Yes, that was a pretty childish reaction for you Cal."

"I'm sorry. I was upset and acted without thought. But I will say now that I have had time to process, I am happy for you Finley. You found your mate." He looked awed by that. "If anyone deserves unconditional love, the completion that comes with finding the other half of their soul, it is you." A small smile on his face as if he was happy for me—as happy as one could be knowing someone they loved would forever be out of reach.

"Where do we go from here?" I asked him.

I wanted to feel angry at him still but something about this long-overdue conversation made me feel lighter. Opening up and talking about the most miserable part of my life, which I usually bottled up, was making me feel better. I also realized I was tired of holding a grudge and being angry and bitter.

"Whether you can find it in you to forgive me or not, we are allies. Someday, I hope we can be friends again as well." Hopeful eyes locked with mine.

Twenty–Six

XAN

The feeling of a warm body slipping from my arm woke me from my sleep. I opened my eyes just a tad and saw Finley trying to sneak out of the room. It was clear she was trying not to wake me, whether that was for my benefit or because she needed some time alone to think was unclear. So, I pretended to be asleep as she snuck away. There have been many changes she's had to deal with lately and having her ex here hasn't been easy on her either, so I could give her this.

Once I was sure she had vacated our floor I slipped out of the bed. I wasn't quite ready to be out of bed yet but there was a lot of planning needed done. I looked at the clock on the nightstand, it wasn't early but earlier than I would normally be awake, it was best to get on with my day, so I grudgingly got dressed.

When I pulled my door open, I came face to face with Hadeon who was leaning on the wall opposite my room. He seemed to know I was about to exit the room and appeared to be waiting for me as he rested one booted foot on the wall behind him, arms crossed, the pose of casual patience.

Not one for mornings I grunted a greeting with the miniscule enthusiasm I could muster.

He surveyed me for a minute before reporting on Callum and Knox's conversation from when he returned from his pity party.

"I talked to Finley already this morning when I caught her downstairs. I thought you might want to know that she's currently hashing things out with Callum." When he told me what was happening, I started to march away, but before I could get far, he snagged my arm, whipping me back around. "I know she's your mate and therefore you are inclined to be possessive and protective to an annoying extent, but they seemed to be having a conversation that is many years in the making. You might let them sort their shit out before you bust in there like a caveman. Maybe if they work things out enough, they can tolerate each other's presence enough for us all to survive this forced confinement together."

As much as I hated it, he was probably right. "Where were they talking?" I think he could tell it was more from curiosity, not the innate desire to go beat the shit out of Callum.

"They were talking on the back porch. I listened in for a bit, so I imagine they won't be too much longer."

I nodded and after thanking him for the information I decided to give Finley a little more time before I tried to intervene.

It was clear if I was planning on not interrupting, I needed a distraction, so I headed to the conservatory to check on my plants for the day.

When I entered the conservatory I went straight to my favorite section, my poisonous plants. It is probably macabre, but I felt a sense of contentment and peace come over me when arrived there. The first thing I did was check the hydroponic station I had assembled for my water hemlock. When I found everything was in working order, I watered the deadly nightshade plants. The black-colored berries of the nightshade were looking quite plump, getting close to the size of a cherry, soon I would need to harvest them. The oleander was in bloom, the flowers vibrant and beautiful.

I was staring at them unintentionally while zoning out, letting my thoughts take control. An arm wrapped around my waist from behind and I knew it was Finley without having to look at her. She hugged me tight, resting her head between my shoulder blades. I let her have a few minutes of comfort from holding me close before addressing the situation with Callum.

"Heard you and Callum were hashing some things out this morning. Want to talk about it?" I asked her as I turned in her arms to face her.

She huffed a small breath out before saying, "Hadeon tell you?"

"Of course."

She chuckled but didn't seem bothered by the revelation. "He's too nosy for his good." She replied to me with a small scowl on her face that I couldn't help laughing at.

"Fine, Callum corned me into talking this morning. At first, I wanted nothing to do with it, but I think it went as well as it could. We both had a lot of things we should have dealt with a long time ago and didn't. So, I guess you could say it was therapeutic in a sense. While I can say with certainty, we will never be best buds I think we worked things out enough that we can be in the same room without killing each other, which should suit this tenuous alliance nicely."

I tightened my hold on her to show my love. Kissing her on the top of the head I told her, "I'm proud of you. I know it is a difficult situation and not something anyone wants to deal with, but you are putting the good of us all above your history with him. Thank you for making the effort to keep the peace."

"Maybe since you are feeling so thankful you can show your appreciation for me later." She smirked with a lascivious look in her eyes. Oh, I certainly would, no asking needed.

With my agreement that she would be getting rewarded later, she took my hand in mine and started leading me to the exit. "We have much to discuss with the others now that everyone is here, let's get it over with."

Twenty–Seven

FINLEY

Xan and I split up, each of us heading in different directions to collect everyone for our meeting which was much overdue. I found Kai pacing around her room in a sulky mood. I tried to extract information about her and Al, but she was still being tight-lipped about whatever happened.

Once I dragged Kai from her room we trudged to the library where everyone else was already waiting for us lounging on the comfy couches. Xan beckoned me to sit with him. When I got situated on the couch next to him, I noticed Kai chose to be as far away from Al as she could get without isolating herself from the conversation.

Hadeon was the only one of us not sitting, he stood in the front of the room facing us. "I've been watching Fallon some, since he doesn't know who I am I figured it would be most beneficial for me to spy on him," Hadeon said. When everyone nodded at him in acknowledgment he continued. "He's being extremely volatile. He's put up wanted posters around town with Finley and Xan's faces and information."

Kai gasped, "That asshole!"

"That's not all," he continued. "He is spreading lies, saying that Finley and Xan were responsible for abducting Knox and Callum. He has many in the pack convinced that you plan to kill his brothers. He showed them what you did to Benny and is saying it's evidence of your ill intent."

"Well shit, that's coming back to bite us in the ass," Kai grumbled.

I had to agree with Kai. While I wasn't regretful of taking Benny out of the game, it didn't help us any that it was being used as evidence against us.

"Sorry," I mumbled to our group, chagrined at the issue I inadvertently caused us.

Xan waved his hand in a manner to dismiss the guilt I felt. He had a smug look about him; he certainly was reveling in the lengths I was willing to go to to rescue him.

I pinched his side, just to let him know I was onto what he was about. All he did was chuckle in response and stare blankly at Hadeon, a picture of perfect concentration.

Hadeon addressed Callum asking for a report of who Callum had reached out to inside the pack and the outcome of those conversations.

"I called several people in the pack. Some were unreachable, or maybe unwilling to call me back, it's unsure. I talked to Derek Grenshaw, he's one of the longest-standing elders for the pack. For those who aren't familiar with pack life, the elders are not official leaders, but they advise the alpha and help keep the peace. He said that Fallon was on a rampage. He's put the pack into a mandatory lockdown and has everyone camping out at our family's property in tents, unwilling to let anyone go to their own homes."

"I guess the property maps and plans will be useful after all," Knox said while unrolling a blown-up enhanced map of the MacGregor estate.

"Good, this will be very helpful," Hadeon addressed to Knox.

"Derek said he would back a coup against Fallon because he is risking the packs' safety and being a general tyrant."

"Did you hear from anyone else?"

"Most were worried about getting involved, even if they don't agree with Fallon and his actions, they are too scared to stand against him. Derek is going to put out some feelers with the other pack elders in secret. He is going to try and get their support for us as well. Having them openly support us will help sway other members to our side."

"Good." Hadeon nodded, looking distant, lost in thought.

"So, what are we going to do?" I asked tentatively.

Knox grinned viciously, "Now we plan a coup."

Twenty-Eight

CALLUM

I thought our attempt at a coup was an obvious solution to our problems since we wanted to take Fallon down. But Knox giving voice to the words seemed to surprise most of the group. Finley who was just taking a sip of an iced coffee suddenly sputtered, sending coffee shooting out of her mouth in every direction. The squatch, Al seemed wary of the idea. Leora, the light faerie, shoots her eyebrows up in surprise. Kai seemed the most enthusiastic of the group, letting out a yell of, "Hell yeah!" Accompanied by a whoop and fist pump in the air.

Hadeon seemed to be thinking over the situation. I knew from what I'd gathered about the group that he became experienced with battle planning at some point in his long immortal lifetime. His eyes were glazed as he stared vacantly for a moment before asking, "Who would take over leadership?"

Knox looked in my direction. I knew he wanted no part of being alpha, that much was obvious when he tried to concede the alpha challenge from the very beginning following our father's death. He was gazing at me expectantly. But to be honest I wasn't the right one for the job either. I've had more than my fair share of fuck ups in my life, and I wasn't the right fit.

Our leader needed to be someone who would be a fair and just leader. Someone who could look at things objectively and always put their people first. We needed someone strong and willing to defend the pack. Someone honorable. These weren't characteristics that were used to describe me.

"I wouldn't be the right fit," I told my brother when he refused to move his expectant eyes away from me.

"Well, I sure as hell don't want to get stuck with the job!" He grumbled angrily in reply. He crossed his arms in front of his chest giving me the stink eye.

"No one said it had to be one of us." My reply made his eyebrows rise in surprise from the shock of my meaning.

"Fang alpha has been a position held by members of our family for generations."

I turned my head away from him and toward the group. "I think it's time for someone else to take over the leadership."

Kai seemed frustrated with the non-answers that have been shared. "Then who?" She practically shouted the question.

I eyed Finley before saying, "I think you should do it."

She gasped. "Me? Have you lost your mind?"

"My mind is quite sound. It's time someone else took over the pack. I think it should be you. You care greatly for the members.

You've shown courage standing up to Fallon and calling out his tyranny. Misogynists wouldn't consider you a threat, but you are one of the strongest in the pack. You would be able to challenge him and have the best chance of winning."

"You're serious?" She asked me with her mouth gaping open. She looked frozen like her mind was glitching from my statement.

"It's a pretty good idea," Kai told her.

Hadeon nodded his head a couple of times before agreeing with my assessment. Al and Leora accepted my idea and offered to help with preparations in any manner that was needed of them. Xan wore a wicked grin before dropping to his knees in front of Finley. He grabbed her hand and bent his head over it, kissing the top before smugly saying, "My mate, the alpha. Sounds fucking hot."

I might have finally accepted their relationship but seeing stuff like this made me want to barf. The touch-feeling crap they were always doing was disturbing. How could two people be so into each other? I guess it should be expected from fate-blessed mates, I haven't met a lot of them before, so it was probably normal for them.

With wide owl-like eyes, she asked no one in particular, "You think I could do it? That I could challenge him and win? That I can be the leader Fang deserves?"

Multiple yells of, "Yes," came from the group. It was settled. Fallon's days as the alpha would be numbered.

Twenty-Nine

FINLEY

After everyone agreed on our plans for me to officially challenge Fallon before the pack as witnesses, we decided it would be imperative for us to have a small reprieve for preparations. We concluded two weeks would be sufficient to make all our arrangements. That two weeks was almost up. Tomorrow would be the day I would challenge Fallon and either fail—keeping everyone trapped under his tyrannical rule— or I would be victorious and usher in a new era for the Fang pack. A change that would break the generations of MacGregors who have been alpha, as well as bring about the first female alpha of Fang.

To say the stakes were high would be an understatement. Therefore, it should not be a surprise to anyone that I might be in a bit of a piss poor attitude. It was a lot of pressure to have on my shoulders, one I wasn't sure I was ready to undertake despite the constant encouragement of my friends who had become like family.

We decided that for our last night of reprieve, we would all eat dinner together. You would think that us all being here in hiding would have led to many shared dinners over the last few weeks but that isn't exactly the truth. For starters, Kai and Al could hardly be in the same room as each other without seeming to want to murder the other. Leora has been playing fairy godmother on the house, using some of her small magics as well as her skill in interior design to help get our delipidated home looking and feeling much grander than when we first arrived. Hadeon was still frequently running out on spying missions to keep tabs on Fallon and the other Fang pack members.

The MacGregor boys were around but for the most part, Callum kept to himself. I could tell he was still trying to figure out where he fits in our group despite us coming to a hesitant truce. While he was more of a loner, Knox was the complete opposite. He had befriended Xan—if someone who didn't know them saw them interact, they would think they had known each other their whole lives. Knox was now an almost permanent fixture in the conservatory helping Xan with the gardening and maintenance of the plants. He had also been fascinated by the poisonous varieties that Xan considered to be his 'specialty'.

Al and Leora were the self-proclaimed best cooks among us, so they did the honors of creating a grand feast for tonight. When I walked towards the dining area the smells wafting through the air made my mouth pool with saliva and my stomach grumble angrily.

The sight of all the food covering the large table made me want to hug both Leora and Al in the tightest possible hugs. Maybe even sings their praises like a bard of old. I would settle for showing my appreciation with words spoken rather than any of the aforementioned dramatics.

My arms were feeling weighed down with the bottles of wine I had retrieved from the basement. Not because they were overtly heavy but because my muscles had been quite sore from all the extra training and sparing, I have been forced to partake in lately. Hadeon had been very adamant about helping me train and let me tell you it's a bitch to try and fight a battle-experienced vampire. Vampire speed is so much quicker than what a shifter can do. The only thing we were probably matched with was strength because both vampires and shifters have increased strength compared to humans.

Setting down the wine bottles on the table I went around and started placing a wine glass at each place setting. By the time I was finished laying them out everyone had gathered together.

I wasn't initially sure where to sit but seeing as everyone else was now seated there was only one remaining seat open. Xan waved me over to the spot and pulled my chair out for me, ever the gentleman—well when he felt like it.

"Don't you want this seat?" I asked him when I saw he was trying to seat me at the head of the table.

"No, I will be right here beside my goddess of a mate." He replied as he gestured to the seat directly to the right of the one, he offered me.

Not feeling like pushing the argument I accepted the offering, and he pushed my chair in until my stomach was flush with the table.

Dinner was surprisingly drama-free. Everyone sat around telling stories or antidotes about their lives that either no one knew or only a few did. Lots of laughing was had, whether that was organic, or the wine contributed to it I was unsure. But I was thankful nonetheless for the good time together.

The end of dinner came quicker than I would have liked and as everyone else headed off to their rooms for the night I was left feeling a little hollow inside. I could have used having a little more time of laughing and merriment to distract me from what tomorrow would bring.

My mate must have sensed this because he knew what I needed. He grabbed my hand pulling me out of my spot and leading me upstairs to our shared room.

As soon as the door shut behind us, he was on me. His lips met mine in a searing kiss. It wasn't a gentle thing, but I think he knew I didn't need gentle, I needed wild.

Without realizing we had even been moving I found myself now on the other side of the room. Xan forcefully turned my face away from him. In the next instance, I was bent over the edge of the bed, my stomach lying against the mattress. Ass flush to his pelvis.

My pants and underwear met the floor, and he squatted down behind me, taking slow languid licks of the evidence of my arousal accumulating at my entrance before moving to lick my clit. His tongue worked in quick flicks, bringing me close to the edge of release before he pulled away.

The groan I released was frustrated and full of the disappointment of him not letting me climax. But before I could dwell long on the problem, he swiftly entered me with a vigorous thrust. His cock slid deep, right where I needed him.

This coupling was much more passionate than our previous ones. We always had the best sex I'd ever had but tonight was even better than usual. There was no containing the lust we felt for each other. We came together with no regard for anyone who might be unfortunate enough to hear us.

He was kissing along the back of my neck, hands braced tightly on both sides, when he thrust hard, throwing me into an orgasm that took me by surprise. It was so powerful that my knees started to buckle. I didn't fall though thanks to Xan maintaining that firm grip.

Now that I fell off the edge Xan was quick to follow. We both stayed like that for a few minutes, catching our breath and trying to regain our composure.

When we finally seemed to gain some semblance of agility again, he slid from me, placing me on the bed. He stuffed his cock back into his pants, which he was still wearing, and straightened to standing.

"Stay here and rest, love. I'll grab a washcloth and get you cleaned."

Before I could formulate a response to him, he was no longer in the room and as hard as I tried, I couldn't keep my eyes open. I fell into the most restful sleep I had ever experienced.

Thirty

XAN

Today would be the day we have been waiting and preparing for. Once we decided to take down Fallon by having Finley challenge him for the position of Alpha, we planned tonight to be the night. The reason has to do with the full moon and that the pack would be having a pack meeting this evening. We planned to be in attendance and use the crowd as witnesses, to make sure he wasn't able to try and lie his way out of it when he loses.

Last night helped Finley get out of her head, unlocking the mental cage she was creating from worry. I helped her relax and after our vigorous activities, she slept like a corpse for the rest of the night. When she woke this morning, she seemed more rested than she had been in weeks. She had a firm resolve that was visible as soon as she rose for the day.

We all had parts to play tonight when we went to the Fang pack lands. Finley had the hardest of the tasks, challenging and winning against Fallon. The rest of us would help with crowd control, basically making sure that none of Fallon's cronies got the idea to try to interfere with the challenge, helping him cheat.

It was almost time to leave. I hadn't been nervous until now. I did not doubt in my mind Finley would win tonight, but being my mate, I was worried for her safety. I didn't want any harm to come to her.

I was just finishing packing up some herbs and plants in a small bag to take with us. It was best to be prepared for anything, so I made sure I had a little of everything in case I needed to use my magic to protect us. Hadeon popped his head through the conservatory door and let me know it was time to head out.

We convened in the driveway around the vehicles. We decided to carpool between two cars to stay close to each other. In one we had Leora, Al, Ry, and Knox. In the other, it was Kai, Hadeon, Callum, Finley, and me.

Not many words were exchanged before we loaded the cars, but silent head nods were given to all. We had this, that was what it meant to us. We were in this together and we would not fail.

It might be a weird turn of events, but we allowed Callum to be the one to drive our vehicle. He knew the way to get there easily. Hadeon thought it was a good idea because he would ride in the passenger seat so he could keep watching with his preternaturally good vampire vision. Making sure that no one caused us to be deterred from our destination.

I kept my arm wrapped tightly around Finley as we sat in the back with Kai. If it wouldn't make the others uncomfortable, I would be doing more than just holding my love, but since it definitely would bother the others, I just held her tight imbuing my touch with as much comfort and confidence as possible.

"We're getting close, it's just around the corner. Elder Grenshaw told me that Fallon has been keeping the path to the house guarded. If you've got any ideas now would be a time to be forthcoming." Callum said to no one in particular.

Now I felt vindicated in my little magical bag of tricks I had brought along. My lips curled in what was probably an evil grin.

Rusting in my bag, I told him, "When we get there the guard will only see you. Since Fallon has been spreading falsities about us abducting you, we'll use that to our advantage. You need to put on the best performance you can, selling them the fake story about you escaping our captivity and just wanting to return to the pack after your ordeal."

Callum gave a grim nod to me in agreeance while I started mixing some of my supplies. "What about the other car?" He asked me, referring to the other half of our comrades who were falling behind us.

"Don't worry about them. They will be shielded too. Just pretend it's only you here."

Kai let the other car know the plan on her phone, so they knew what to expect.

When we were almost to the property but still out of sight Callum told me it was time to enact my magic. Rolling my window down I tossed my concoction out the open window so that it hit the car behind us. I then tossed some of the mixture on everyone except Callum and mumbled the spell that would keep the rest of us hidden.

Shortly after we rolled up to the drive, which was guarded by several shifters.

They yelled for Callum to stop the car, which he obliged, putting the car in park.

He rolled his window down. The rest of us stayed quiet while he elaborated on the woes of being abducted, lightly tortured, and his harrowing escape from the Finley and her 'evil' warlock who had brainwashed her. He was a much better actor than I would have expected, he would have seemed believable if I didn't know it was all bullshit.

"Oh shit!" One of the shifters responded to his tale. "We got to get him to the healer stat to be looked over and notify Fallon of his return."

They ushered Callum to proceed, and we entered undetected along with our other car.

Still shielded, I slid from the car that was barely rolling down the drive and I looped back around to the guards. Taking a potion from my bag, I tossed it in the center of the guards. When it landed on the ground it exploded in a cloud of colorful smoke. The potion was a sedative and knocked all of the guards into an unwilling slumber. They would not be an issue for the next few hours or so. We wouldn't need to worry about them notifying Fallon of Callum's arrival.

Now that the guards were taken care of, I jogged ahead and jumped back into the car that was still creeping forward.

"The witnesses will be down for a couple of hours. No one will be the wiser. Let's go infiltrate this meeting." I told them.

Callum finally hit the gas and drove us to the house. The front was filled with cars. Tents were lining the sides of the house, evidence of the truth the elder told Callum, about Fallon keeping most of the pack secluded here.

The car was put in park and before the engine was even switched off our doors were flung open as we climbed out.

Hadeon and Callum took up the lead as we rounded the house, to approach the backyard where the meeting would be taking place.

The sunsetting, allowed gold to surround us all, it made Finley look like she was crowned by light. She had never looked more beautiful than now, the glow of her skin, and violence in her eyes.

As we emerged and started walking through the crowd they started murmuring and stepping aside, probably from shock.

As we made it to the front of the crowd, we were able to lay eyes on Fallon, who had a shifter tied up, beating the shit out of him. So, it would seem the rumor of him acting violently toward the pack was the truth.

He was able to punch the shifter in the face again when his fist stopped its forward motion, and he noticed us. The shock was the first emotion that crossed his face, but he was quickly rid of it, fury taking over in its place.

"Ah, if it isn't my beloved brothers returned to us once more." The words were said as if he missed his brothers, but his tone lacked the emotion of actually meaning it. He seemed to know that his brothers were never being held by us, that they were with us willingly.

His gaze turned to Finley. It was a lecherous thing. If I didn't know the world of pain Finley planned for him, I would be on him in a minute. She was mine to look at, he didn't deserve to lay his eyes on her.

"And my future mate as well." He said smugly. "What an honor to have you all home where you belong."

A growl ripped from Finley, "I am not, and will never be your mate." She seethed.

"Then why have you returned?" He asked, arms outstretched like he thought he was some ancient ruler holding court.

"I am here for one reason and one reason only," she said quietly. Getting louder she announced, "I am here to challenge you for alpha of Fang." Her voice rang out loudly across the entirety of the yard. Gasps and murmurs broke free at her pronouncement.

Thirty-One

CALLUM

Fallon scoffed following Finley's pronouncement of the challenge. He sneered in her direction, "Do you think you can beat me?" He looked completely crazed as he threw his head back and laughed at this like it was an amusing joke.

"Yes, I can and will beat you," Finley exclaimed, full of confidence.

Fallon stopped laughing then. He turned and pinned her with a seething glare. "Why are you doing this Fin? We can finally be together. I was offering to give you everything. Why can't you just accept me? We could be happy together I know it."

"I've was never interested in you in that way, Fallon. You were my best friend at one point. You were one of the best things in my life. But you threw it away. Then you become alpha and think that entitles you to be able to force me into becoming your mate." She turns to the side, pulling her hair back she reveals the claiming mark on her neck. "I have a mate."

Fallon narrows his eyes seeing the mark and lets out a ferocious growl before stalking towards her with stomping feet. He starts circling her angrily and tries to grab her. She dodges and slips away from him.

"You've forced my hand, Fallon. You are not fit to lead Fang. Accept the challenge," she demanded.

He throws his arms out, holding them up he turns slowly in a circle. "Well? Do you all think I need to fight Finley?" He yells to the crowd who are all eyeing him warily.

The pack members all started nodding and approving of the challenge. When it seemed like he failed to get the answer he wanted he looked more furious than when we first arrived.

"Fine, have it your way," he tells her in a rough gravelly tone. "But know this, there will be no submission. It's a challenge to the death. Do you still wish to challenge me?"

"I'd rather not kill you. But if it is to the death, you require then yes. The challenge still stands." Finley held her head high looking like a fierce warrior.

"Then let us have a challenge ring set up." Fallon snapped at some of his sycophants to get a circle set up to contain the fight.

When the circle was drawn in a barren patch of the yard Finley flagged Xan to her. She pointed to the circle while speaking too quietly for anyone to hear.

He walked to the circle while digging through the satchel of magical supplies he brought with him. When he had a handful of something he started walking the line, sprinkling the dried ingredients while chanting in a language I couldn't understand.

"What are you doing?" Fallon yelled at Xan. Trying to interrupt his process. When he started moving toward Xan like he might go after him physically, I inserted myself between the two. I stood guard while Xan finished laying whatever spell Finley had asked for.

"He put a spell on the challenge circle. No contestant will be able to cross the border without the challenge being complete." Finley sounded like this should be obvious.

It was a good idea. It would keep them from creating chaos around the yard or accidentally hurting any bystanders. While also making sure no one can try to run away from the fight.

"Let's get this over with," she stated walking into the challenge ring.

Begrudgingly Fallon entered on the opposite side. They sized each other up for a couple of minutes, neither making the first move before Fallon said, "Come on Fin, we both know you won't be able to kill me. I mean too much to you." He smirked like he was so sure of that statement's validity.

He truly was delusional. Ever since he burned Finley, she has gone out of her way to stay away from him and have nothing to do with him. He was mentally unwell if he was this insistent that she had feelings for him.

"You have overestimated the value I hold for you." As soon as she replied, she lunged in his direction, changing mid-air into her wolf form.

Caught off guard by her sudden advancement, he shifted to his wolf as well but was slower in doing so. She was able to get a good bite of his arm in the process. When he was shifted, she was still attached to that front leg, and he was letting out an involuntary whimper from the pain.

Snarling he was able to wrestle his arm free but the damage from the bite was already done. He was limping now. That would hurt his chances going forward.

I knew the challenge was necessary, but I wish he wasn't an idiot to insist on a death match. He's been crazy recently and shouldn't be the pack alpha, but he is still my brother, I would prefer for him not to die. But he did insist on fighting to the death, therefore if the challenge ended with Finley winning, I would not have any ill will towards her for killing him.

He tried to lurch at Finley, but she was faster at dodging out of his path since he was hurt. He ended up hitting the ground hard in the spot she was previously standing. An animalistic oomph came from him when he hit the hard ground. Getting back up his limp seemed to worsen.

They were a ball of fur and snarling teeth as they rolled around. Neither seemed to be able to get a secure grip on the other.

Just when it was starting to feel like they were equally matched Finley was able to knock Fallon to the ground. Pinning him down with her open mussel, she tried to get him to submit.

Despite Fallon saying there would be no option for the loser to submit, Finley was still offering my brother mercy after everything he'd done to her. He refused and his struggle intensified.

She kept holding him down. Her wolf head came up and she looked around the crowd. She seemed to lock eyes with me. I could read the look she was giving me. She felt guilty about what was to come and was checking on me.

I knew she wouldn't have a choice. If she let him go and he got the advantage he would kill her. He felt scorned by whatever fairytale romance he made up in his head. He wouldn't quit until she was dead. No, she couldn't do anything except kill him. She knew it and she still was making the offer to me.

There was nothing to be done. I gave her a solemn nod, encouraging her to end it.

With my agreeance, she quit just restraining him. She locked her fangs around his neck and bit down hard. With a loud *crack* permeating the air, my brother fell still, and the challenge was over.

Everyone seemed stunned and silent at first. But as she changed back to her human form thuds sounded throughout the whole clearing as shifters all dropped to one knee, showing their fealty to their new leader. While the death of a pack member was always sad, there were mixed emotions tonight. Fallon hadn't done right by the pack, but he would still be mourned.

Epilogue

FINLEY

***O**ne Month Later*

"Wave them through," I holler to Hadeon who is manning the gate at the driveway entrance. He opens it up and instructs the driver where to go.

Tonight is the first official pack meeting since I became the alpha of Fang. With both Xan's apartment and my home destroyed we decided to establish the Wimbleton Estate as our primary residence.

Surprisingly, all of our inner circle decided to continue living here as well. We've always had a tight-knit group, but since the end of the alpha challenge we have grown even closer—like one big dysfunctional family.

The residence has become our point of command for all pack business. Xan even surprised me recently by redecorating the library room in a style I love; he said that a powerful leader deserved a stylish domain to rule from.

Knox and Callum decided to stay but they insisted on living separately from the main house. They had a small cabin constructed on the acreage where they reside together. It was a surprisingly quick build, but it seemed they had connections to the right people to get it done quickly.

Warm hands slide around my waist, wrapping me in a hug from behind. Xan. My shoulders, which have felt the weight of all these recent changes, release their tension while I'm in his comforting embrace.

"I think that was the last of them if you are ready to address your people." He murmurs in my ear as he nuzzles my neck.

When I nod, he releases me. Taking my hand, we walk around back to where the Fang pack has congregated.

My heart swells at the sight of so many gathered together—not just wolf shifters. Once I took over as alpha, I made changes to our organization. We are now the first pack in history to have supernaturals outside of our species.

As I look out among the crowd, I see so many different species represented here—vampires, a few faeries, sulkies, satyrs, centaurs, witches, warlocks, and our very own sasquatch. Tears start to well in my eyes as I survey all that we have accomplished. It's truly beautiful.

When I decided to be all-inclusive with our membership, I faced a considerable amount of backlash from a few current members of the pack but also some of the outside organizations. When you do something that's never been done sometimes it makes other people uneasy. But change always starts with someone and I decided it was going to be us. A few members of the pack voluntarily revoked their membership in favor of moving to a different pack. Most however were convinced to welcome these changes with open arms.

If not for my friends I would not be here today as pack alpha, Fallon would potentially still be ruling with an iron fist. They were there for me in the hard times, they took risks to help me and my mate. They deserved the sense of family and belonging that comes with being part of a pack. So, it was a no-brainer for me to let them be part of that change.

Xan helps wherever he can and supports me in all my endeavors. He keeps me level-headed and acts as a sounding board for me to bounce my ideas and policies against.

Kai is my number two. She helps with a lot of the paperwork that I wasn't aware would be required of pack leadership. Her superior organizational skills have been a significant boon to me.

Hadeon preferred no official title—however, he is my ears on the ground. He also makes sure our security is top-notch and the pack remains protected.

Ry and Leora volunteered to help with the upkeep of the conservatory as well as the newer gardens that have been planted since making this our home. They also are great at being a friendly face for members to bring concerns to and get help.

Al has been helping get the estate into not just livable condition, but he has gone above and beyond to make this place pristine. It hardly resembles the dilapidated mess we started with. Going forward he is going to be working on setting up some smaller dwellings around the property for guests or any members who might need a temporary residence in the future.

Knox and Callum have been working with the youth of the pack. They are helping the teenage shifters learn about controlling their shifts and teaching them about pack life.

We have a great thing going on here and despite the highs and lows to come, I hope there are great things ahead for our pack—our family.

The End

Want More?

Are you still curious about what happened between Kai and Al? Wonder no more! Read on to get a special bonus chapter from Kai.

Bonus Chapter

KAI

Shit. It's been the only word that's been at the forefront of my mind since the day that I met Alder, Al as his friends call him. Friends—something we are not.

The first time I saw him I knew what we were, and I've been dreading any interaction with him since. I've been trying my best to avoid him, which I'm finding hard to do since we are both an important part of this group of renegades who hope to take down Fallon.

Now that we are at the estate it's even worse. It seems like he's everywhere I turn, everywhere I look.

I've tried being mean. I've tried being hateful. I've tried worse—being completely indifferent. But he doesn't seem to be scared away easily.

I might be the one who introduced Finley to that Mate Match dating app she used to find Xan. But I only ever used it with the intention of hook-ups, never actually intending to find a mate. Barf. I enjoy my singledom and everything that comes with it.

But the minute that absurdly large, woodland creature, known as a sasquatch—who's practically allergic to everything about the outdoors—I knew. I met my mate. And let me tell you, I find him lacking.

Sure, he possesses rugged good looks. He looks like a freaking statuesque mountain man. But he could die from a bazillion different things that could be found in anyone's backyard.

So, like I said, I've done everything I can to avoid him or push him away. I'm not interested. But now he and I have been assigned the task of helping clean up this place. We are supposed to work *together*.

I snapped at him telling him a room he should start with, mainly just to get him away from me so I don't make any stupid decisions and accidentally tie myself to him forever.

It was working great too. But now here he is again.

"I'm finished with the rooms you assigned me, *Your Majesty,*" he says to me in a mocking tone.

Shit. It's all my brain can conjure now that this is the last room we need to finish. We are going to be stuck here together getting the library room ready for our group to meet in.

Without saying anything I turn away from him. I start dusting shelves. He seems to take the hint and decide on something to help with—if the sounds of furniture scraping the floors is any indicator.

The room's finally presentable and I feel the need to flee. Get out of here fast. The need to get away from Al and this confining space as quickly as possible.

I feel like I'm going to hyperventilate from suffocation if I don't escape right this instant.

I turn to flee and of course, bump straight into Al with the full force of my fight-or-flight instincts. He was unprepared to be bulldozed by me and we tumbled to the ground in a heap of tangled limbs.

"Uhh, get off me!" I yell at him, trying to untangle myself.

"You're the one on top of me!" He yells back.

Shit. He's right. I'm lying directly on top of his chest. Deflect, that's all I can do now. So, I try, "Whatever. Get your hands off me." I snap back while bracing my hands on his chest to push off him. Only when my hands connect with his chest do I feel the warm solid muscle of his abs. My fingers start rubbing and scrunching into the muscles without my knowledge.

"It seems a lot like you're the one touching me, not the other way around, *Princess.*" He sneers.

I look down and find that he's right. If my hands weren't touching his delicious muscles, I would face-palm myself right now. This is ridiculous. But I can't seem to move them away. I'm quite enjoying touching him. I'd enjoy it even more if it was anyone but *him.*

I shake my head at myself, unable to make a coherent thought to respond to his taunting.

I think to myself, *I can't let this happen, I don't want this. I can't have a mate.*

Al starts shaking below me as he laughs riotously. Apparently, in my delirium, it wasn't in my head, I said it out loud. Now I do a facepalm. "So, you do know." He states.

Of course, he had to know. I couldn't have gotten lucky and him not know that we were mates. I had hoped it could be a secret only I would keep. But nooooo.

I start squirming because now I don't know what do to and I am about to panic now, knowing that he knows, and he knows that I know.

He snatches me around the waist. What the— "Stop wiggling like that on top of me, unless you find me less repulsive than you have been letting on." There's such a serious look in his eyes as he says it.

Of course, now that he hinted at it, my mind is automatically drawn to visions of us tangling together in an intimate nature. I try to banish the thoughts, but they won't seem to willingly disperse.

He smirks. "Ah, maybe you like the idea of what you are doing to me. You just don't want to like it."

I swallow hard, maintaining eye contact. "Maybe," slips unbidden from my lips in a breathy tone.

His eyes go wide. He was baiting me, it's clear he didn't expect me to react to it. Well, me neither buddy.

His body stiffens for a moment before he seems to decide something. Then in a firm voice, he tells me, "If you want me to make you feel good, go stand by the arm of the couch."

I know exactly what he is planning and offering me. I want desperately to say fuck off and run out of here. But I can't bring myself to do it. I find my feet moving toward the couch. I do as he says and stand by the edge of the couch, but I take it a step further. I lean over and brace my hands on the couch.

I turn and look over my shoulder seeing him stalk towards me full of masculine pride. It lights a fire in me, and I grit out, "One time only." I don't want him getting ideas that I'm instantly all in with him or something. It's just curiosity and arousal. That's it, not the mate thing.

"I'm sure," he whispers against my neck. His hands ran down my sides.

I remember telling him there was a condom in my purse and him grabbing it. He tore it open, but I was too impatient to deal with his fumbling as he was trying to unwrap it. I snatched it and rolled it on his erection before turning back around and bracing myself against the couch.

He reached down checking to see if I was wet. He discovered my most horrible secret—I was flooded. He lined up with my entrance and in one hard thrust entered me. He didn't act delicately as he started rocking in and out.

He worked hard behind me, while holding my blond hair in a tight fist, holding me exactly where he wanted me. After a few minutes of his rough ministrations, we both experienced ecstasy. It was better than anything I had ever experienced before.

This male that I looked down on, perceiving as weak was feral when he pleased me. He was so bossy and commanding—the opposite of the way I had seen him behave around everyone else. It wasn't usually what I was into but damn it worked, and it worked well.

After the glow of an excellent orgasm faded, I stiffened. What the hell did I just do? I felt suddenly mortified. I shouldn't have done this. I have never wanted mate, finding out I have one wouldn't change that.

He seemed to realize how things changed, where my mind went, and the regret I felt. He pulled away and disposed of the full condom in a small bin.

He didn't say anything and neither did I. My mind was blank, all except that one word, the one I've thought over and over since meeting him—*shit.*

Just as we were righting ourselves my best friend in the entire world waltzed in. She stopped in the doorway for a second seeming to assess. Then it became very clear from her facial expression that she realized what had just taken place.

I was in no way ready to confess what happened or why. So, I turned to her and with gritted teeth, I said, "Not. One. Single. Word."

About the Author

Savanna Golden is an author from the Midwest. When not spending time with her husband and five kids she can be found with a book in hand. Her favorite genres to read are romance and fantasy. Her favorite romance trope is enemies to lovers and her least favorite is tied between second chance and miscommunication.

Want to get social? Scan for all of Savanna's important links:

FINDING
Home
SAVANNA GOLDEN

When Rafael's dying father dropped the bombshell that he planned to give his shares of their co-owned baseball team to his irresponsible younger brother, Rafael knew he had to act fast. But when he discovers that his estranged brother has been hiding a divorce and neglecting his children, Rafael sees a chance to save his father's legacy and protect his future

.Jenny is a single mother struggling to make ends meet after her ex-husband's betrayal. When Rafael, her ex's brother, swoops in with a proposal to help them both, she's hesitant but desperate. They agree to a marriage of convenience until Rafael's father passes away, but as they spend more time together, they begin to question if their arrangement is truly temporary.